"I'm not a very **Regina admitt**

"You don't need physical strength to defend yourself," Riley explained. "But you have to stop worrying about other people watching you. So from now on I'm going to give you very private lessons. Just the two of us."

"But, Riley, mostly it's you I worry about." Regina paused, then blurted, "Are you attracted to me?"

"Yes."

"I'm attracted to you, too, and it bothers me, the idea of you seeing me all messy and sweaty."

Riley wanted to see her mussed. He wanted to see her sweat. Hearing her say it sharpened his desire. "Eventually I'll see you every way there is." His gaze never wavered from hers. "And when we have sex you'll definitely be sweaty. Messy, too. That's the way it is with good sex. But I'm willing to bet you'll look hot as hell...."

Dear Reader,

You met Riley Moore in the *Men of Courage* anthology. Now you'll get to know him even better as Riley stakes a claim on his own ladylove. But first he has to ensure her safety from a threat, and convince the lady that he's the only man for her. Of course, the fact that he understands—and even likes!—her little dog is a major plus. Butch is as fiercely protective and loyal as Riley himself, which gives the two snarling, dominating males something in common.

While I never write about actual people I know, I'll confess that Butch is a replica of my own little four-pound Chihuahua, Brock. Around my house, Brock rules—or at least he likes to think he does. He's worked his way right into our hearts. (That's Brock on the inside cover photo with me.) I hope you enjoy Riley, Regina and Butch's tale! Do let me know what you think. You can reach me at lorifoster1@juno.com.

All my best,

Lori Foster

Books by Lori Foster

HARLEQUIN TEMPTATION
852—TREAT HER RIGHT
856—MR. NOVEMBER

HARLEQUIN SINGLE TITLE
CAUGHT IN THE ACT
ONCE AND AGAIN*
FOREVER AND ALWAYS*
CASEY*

*The Buckhorn Brothers

LORI FOSTER

RILEY

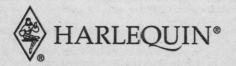

HARLEQUIN®

TORONTO • NEW YORK • LONDON
AMSTERDAM • PARIS • SYDNEY • HAMBURG
STOCKHOLM • ATHENS • TOKYO • MILAN • MADRID
PRAGUE • WARSAW • BUDAPEST • AUCKLAND

To Ellie Davis.
It wasn't that long ago that I didn't have a computer.
Heck, I didn't even own a typewriter. I just knew that I wanted to
write, somehow, someway. It's still incredible to me that you so very
generously typed up my first handwritten manuscript. What a
rambling mess of a story that was—but you didn't tell me so.
Instead, you encouraged me, in more ways than I can say. I
sometimes wonder if I'd be a writer today if you hadn't done me
such an enormous favor. From the bottom of my heart, thank you.
You're one of the good ones.
Love ya!

ISBN 0-373-69130-0

RILEY

Copyright © 2003 by Lori Foster.

This edition published by arrangement with Harlequin Books S.A.

® and TM are trademarks of the publisher. Trademarks indicated with
® are registered in the United States Patent and Trademark Office, the
Canadian Trade Marks Office and in other countries.

Visit us at www.eHarlequin.com

Printed in U.S.A.

1

"RAISE YOUR KNEES."

Wide-eyed, breathless and straining, she said, "No," in such a scandalized voice that Riley Moore grinned. That was the thing about Red—she made him laugh, made him feel lighthearted when he hadn't thought such a thing would be possible ever again. Not a bad start.

But he had other things to accomplish here besides smiling.

"I'm not letting you up till you do." Hell, he'd be happy to stay put for hours. Not only did she amuse him, she also aroused him more than any woman he'd ever known. Her body was slight but very soft, a nice cushion under his larger, harder frame. And the warmth he felt in the cradle of her thighs could drive him over the edge.

Her big green eyes darted left and right. "Riley, people are *watching*."

"I know." He decided to taunt her. After all, this was important. She needed to learn how to handle him. No sense in wasting all his instruction. "They're waiting to see if you've learned anything through all these lessons. Most of them think not. Others are pretty damn doubtful."

New determination drew her slim auburn brows

down into a frown and turned her green eyes stormy. Suddenly her knees were along his sides, catching him off guard with the carnality of it. While his mind wandered down a salacious path, she bucked, rolled—and onto his back he went.

Proud as a peahen, she bounced on his abdomen and cheered herself. Wrong move, sweetheart, he thought, and deftly flipped her straight back and into the same position that she'd just escaped, except that this time her legs were trapped around his waist. With the wind temporarily knocked out of her, she gasped.

Half frustrated, half amused, Riley straightened. Because he knew his own ability, even if most others didn't, he always utilized strict control and caution. Especially with women, and most especially with Red. He'd sooner break his own leg than ever bruise her.

He pulled her upright, forced her arms straight up high to help her breathe, and shook his head. "When you get the upper hand on an attacker, honey, you do not stop to congratulate yourself."

Seeing that the display was over, the crowd dispersed, going back to their own training. Riley stood and gently pulled Regina Foxworth to her feet. She wasn't necessarily a short woman, but next to his height, she seemed almost puny. The top of her head reached his shoulder. Her wrists were like chicken bones. Narrow shoulders, a delicate frame...and yet, she wanted him to teach her self-defense.

Riley snorted. Hell, whenever he got this close to her he had things other than fighting on his mind. And the fact that, regardless of what he'd tried to teach her, she still ended up on her back with him in the mounted position put all kinds of considerations in his mind.

Like what it'd be like to have her situated that way, with no clothes between them and without her attempting to escape.

Soon, he promised himself. Very soon.

In a huff, Regina promptly jerked away and began straightening her glorious red hair. If the woman thought half as much about applying herself as she did about her appearance, they'd make more progress.

For her lessons today she'd restrained her hair in a braid as thick as his wrist that hung to the middle of her back. Already silky tendrils had worked loose, giving her a softened, just-laid look. Riley shook his head in awe. He worked with other women and they just got sweaty and rumpled. Not Regina. Somehow, no matter what, the woman always managed to look more appealing.

Watching her tidy her braid sent tension rippling through his muscles. A man could conjure quite a few fantasies over that hair, not to mention the delicate, ultrafeminine body that came with it. Hell, he even found the sprinkling of freckles over her nose adorable.

Riley snatched up a towel. "Quit pouting, Red."

"I'm not." But her bottom lip stuck out in a most becoming way. Normally a princess like her wouldn't have appealed to him. But Red had guts beneath the fussy exterior. And in the time he'd known her, he'd also realized she was gentle, compassionate, understanding, and damn it, he wanted her, had from the very start.

If that had been his only problem, he'd have coaxed her into bed by now. But it was more than that. He hadn't thought to ever want involvement with another woman, but he wanted it with Red.

Riley slung his arm around her shoulders and headed her toward the shower. Not that she needed to shower. The natural fragrance of her skin and hair was warm and womanly. His body tensed a bit more in masculine awareness, on the verge of cramping. "We're wasting our time with these lessons."

"I need to be able to defend myself."

True enough. Three weeks ago, Regina had been caught in a burning building while on assignment for the *Chester Daily Press.* As a reporter, she liked to stick her cute little freckled nose into places where it didn't belong, and that particular building had been in a disreputable part of town. That should have been her first clue not to be there. The fact that the fireworks dealer had already had trouble in the past should have been her second.

She'd forged on anyway and had come damn close to dying for her efforts. Most were inclined to call the fire an accident due to the shoddy management of the owner, who left opened pyrotechnics scattered around. But there was more to it. Long before Red got caught up in that fire, she'd been afraid. Riley first met her while she attempted to interview his friend, Ethan, for commendable work as a firefighter. Even then, she'd been as jumpy as a turkey on Thanksgiving morning. She'd seemed so strained, Riley had expected her to scream at any minute.

The day after the interview, she'd come into his gym

and asked for lessons to protect herself. Unlike most of the women who approached him with the same request, Red had seemed more desperate, as if she needed the lessons for an imminent threat, not for general assurances.

Before the fire, he'd discarded her claims of endangerment, as had the county police where he worked as an evidence tech. *They* still didn't believe her, but at thirty-two, through life and some hard lessons, Riley had learned to read people, to sift real from feigned. Red was afraid, and he'd bet she had reason.

Someone was after her. She didn't know why. He didn't care why.

The day she'd almost died in that fire, he'd staked a claim. Little Red just hadn't figured that out yet. But no way in hell would he let anyone hurt her.

"Why don't you shower up and we'll talk about it?"

"Again?" She gave her long-suffering look. "There's nothing more to say. The police don't believe me, nothing else major has happened—"

Riley jumped on her choice of words. "What do you mean, nothing major? Has something minor happened?"

She shrugged, which did interesting things to her petite breasts. Dressed in snug biker shorts and a matching sports tank, there wasn't much of her body left to his imagination. But then, he'd wrestled with her enough and studied her in such detail that Riley already knew she had a discreet rack. Her breasts were small, firm and a definite draw to his eyes.

He could span her waist easily in his big hands, but from there she flared out. Her bottom was fuller, nicely rounded, as he liked. Not that it mattered. He already knew you couldn't judge the woman by the package. A facade of innocence, of kindness, or honor, meant nothing, less than nothing.

Regina could have looked a dozen different ways and he'd still want her because her draw on him went deeper than appearances. He felt an affinity to her, a vague basis he could trust in and that, more than anything, appealed to him. It seemed the moment he'd met her something had sparked.

So far, she'd shut him out.

"My apartment door was vandalized the other day."

Riley stopped dead in his tracks, right in front of the entrance to the women's shower. In a voice low with annoyance and disbelief, he growled, "Why the hell didn't you tell me?"

"I'm telling you now."

"Now is too damn late." He felt like shaking her, but she was so dainty a good shake would rattle her teeth.

"There were three other doors that got egged, so I figured it was random, not personal. And really, there's no threat in an egging, just an aggravation."

"Unless someone is trying to bug you enough to make you move." The fact that she lived in a nice apartment building with good security and lots of neighbors around reassured Riley many a night. It was the only thing that had kept him from forcing his pursuit of her. Because he felt she was safe at night, he intended to let her get used to him at her own pace. Little by little, he'd make his intentions known.

Still, he felt compelled to point out the facts. "I don't

care what *you* figured, Red. From now on, tell me everything. I'm the expert here."

Her gaze dipped over his chest, now damp with sweat so that his T-shirt stuck to him. Wrestling with her hadn't caused any exertion, but he'd been in the private studio all morning giving lessons. Besides, just being near Red fired his blood. Having her open and vulnerable beneath him brought out a possessive sweat. He'd conquer her—in his own time.

"Yes, you're an expert, Riley." Staring up at him, her big eyes full of serious regard, she added, "At a lot of things."

"At a..." His voice trailed off. Was she coming on to him? 'Bout damn time. He crowded closer to her, letting her feel the heat of his body, instinctively overpowering her with his size and masculinity and interest. "Just what does that mean, Regina?" He sounded gruff, half-aroused, but then she had that effect on him.

Head tipped way back to meet his gaze, she sighed. "You're an amazing guy, Riley Moore. That's all I meant. I don't know any other man who used to be part of a SWAT team, now serves as a crime scene evidence technician, *and* owns his own gym."

Deflated, mouth flat, Riley said, "No."

With a ludicrous show of innocence, she blinked. "No, what?"

"No, I won't do the damn interview." He should have seen right through her. He was good at deciphering motives, but his perspective was blown around her, clouded by lust. She'd been after an interview for over a week now, but his past was just that: the past.

He wouldn't dredge it up for anyone, not even Little Red.

"But—"

At that moment, Rosie Winters shoved her way out of the showers, forcing them both to back up. Now Rosie, bless her, knew how to work out. She got sweaty, red-faced and hot. *Not* more appealing. She cursed, grunted, struggled, and she gave it her all, showing constant improvement without a single thought to her hair or audience.

Like Riley, Rosie fought to win and she was now good enough that she just might stand a chance against a man without Riley's special training. But as ex-SWAT, Riley could be lethal when necessary. His job had taught him how to come out the victor in any scenario. But long before that, when he'd still been a kid, nature had taught him that he didn't like to lose.

At anything.

As one of his best friends, Rosie had been coming to his gym a lot, much to Ethan's dismay. She and Ethan had married last week, but that hadn't slowed down Rosie. Nothing slowed her down. The newlyweds supplied endless hours of entertainment with the way they clashed wills, and the way they loved.

"Hey, Riley." Rosie gave him a resounding smooch on the cheek before turning to Regina. Her brown hair, still wet, hung down her back. "I lingered in the shower so I could talk to you."

Regina lifted her brows. "Really? What about?"

"Prepare yourself," Rosie warned with a lot of suspenseful anticipation. "Your loan went through. You're all set to close on the house!"

That announcement seemed to set off both women. Regina squealed as females are wont to do, and Rosie, who never squealed, laughed heartily. But around Regina, Rosie often got pulled into the more feminine mannerisms. Like now, with Regina holding her hands and dancing in circles and bouncing around.

Watching them, Riley crossed his arms and leaned back against the wall. He just adored women, the way they reacted, their expressions, their unique mindset that was so different from men's. Rosie and Regina couldn't be more dissimilar in most ways, yet they had similarities, too, just by virtue of being female.

It gave him pleasure to listen in—until it dawned on him what Rosie had said. He shoved away from the wall. "A house? You bought a house?"

They quieted, but both still grinned hugely. "It's adorable," Regina confided. "Just the right size for me."

"And such a great bargain," Rosie added. "Because it's empty, she can have immediate occupancy."

"Immediate occupancy?" The words emerged a dark whisper. "As in alone in a house, unprotected, immediately?"

Rosie paused. "Oh. I hadn't thought of that. I mean, it's in a nice quiet neighborhood with half-acre yards—"

"Great. Just great."

Regina gave him a level look. "Really, Riley. You act like I'll be camping in the open with wild bears all around me. I can lock my doors and windows." When he only narrowed his eyes, she added, "I'll even buy an alarm system, okay?"

"It's a lousy idea. Have you two forgotten that some-one recently tried to burn you alive?"

Rosie shuddered. "I'll never forget." She'd gone with Regina that day, and damn near died because of it. "But the police seem to think that it was either van-dalism that got out of hand, negligence on the part of the owner, or at the very worst, vengeance aimed at the owner, not at us."

Regina watched Riley closely. "They think we were innocent bystanders."

"Right. And that's why your camera was taken and the owner has disappeared?"

Looking guilty, Rosie turned to Regina. "Maybe he's right."

"No, he is not right. I have to live somewhere, so it might as well be my own house." She patted Riley on the chest. Though she did it negligently, without a sin-gle sign of awareness on her part, he felt the damn pat clear through to his masculine being. "I'll get an alarm system *and* a dog. How's that?"

Seeing that he wouldn't win, Riley gave up that par-ticular argument. At least she wanted to take steps in the right direction. A big, well-trained German shep-herd or Doberman would certainly be a deterrent to anyone thinking to harm her. In the meantime, he'd just have to see about advancing his courtship. Once she gave in, he'd have the right to keep her close, to watch over her.

And all her spare time would be spent in bed, giving her less time to get into trouble.

With Ethan and Rosie's rushed wedding plans, they'd been forced together more frequently than otherwise. Adding to that her lessons at the gym, he'd seen her almost daily for the past three weeks. Their time together had been platonic because he couldn't possibly wrestle with her and have romantic thoughts without embarrassing them both, and possibly breaking a few sexual harassment laws. He felt certain a boner would have been out of line.

But he knew how he felt. Maybe it was time she knew, too.

It wouldn't be a bad idea to live with her until he felt secure that she'd be safe alone. The benefits to that scenario were more than obvious. To both of them.

"When's the closing on the house?"

Rosie winced.

Resigned, Riley asked again, "How soon, Rosie?"

"Weeeelll..." Rosie cast a quick look at Regina, but she was too busy smiling over her good news to share Rosie's uncertainty. "Because the house was empty and her credit impeccable, I sort of rushed it through. We have a date set for the middle of next week."

Regina squealed again, but with Riley so subdued, she quickly quieted. "You're being such a stick in the mud, Riley. Can't you be just a little happy for me?"

If it weren't such bad timing, he would be. But he worried about her enough already without her being off on her own, away from the safety of the apartment complex. In his mind, she was already his. He wanted to protect her, not leave her safety dependent on a dog and alarm.

He studied her for a long moment, deciding how best to proceed without making her more skittish. Then he realized his stare alone had her squirming un-

comfortably. He tried a smile, but it felt more preda-
tory than anything else. "I'll take you to dinner to cel-
ebrate." He made it a statement rather than an
invitation, on the off chance she thought to refuse.

Her hesitation fell heavy between them. "I don't
know…"

Riley took a step closer. "Say yes, Regina."

Rosie's gaze bounced back and forth, watching them
with great interest.

A blush tinged Regina's cheeks. "The thing is, I
wanted to get my dog today. I figure I might as well
potty train him at my apartment so he won't mess up
my house."

Riley didn't let her off the hook. He waited, still
watching her intently until her unease was palpable.

Finally, she sighed. "If you can come over around
six, I can cook dinner at my place."

Now that sounded promising. Much better suited to
his purpose than being in a crowded restaurant. "I'm
on vacation for the next two weeks, so I'm at your dis-
posal." He realized suddenly that Rosie had a vacuous
grin on her face. She knew him better than Regina did,
so she'd probably already realized how territorial he
felt.

Glancing over his shoulder at the workout area of
the gym, he said, "I have to get back on the floor. I have
three more hours of personal instruction before I'm
free." He touched Regina's cheek. "Promise me you'll
be careful, Red."

She blinked, then stepped out of reach. Her laugh
sounded forced. "It's the middle of the day. I swear, Riley, you're more fretful than I am."

That's because he knew firsthand the danger that could befall a woman alone. He shook off that dark thought and raised her chin. "Promise?"

"Cross my heart." With a last platonic pat on his chest, she said, "Don't be late."

Riley watched her disappear into the shower room, spellbound until Rosie started snickering. When he gave her his attention, she clutched her heart and pretended to swoon.

"Brat." Riley put her in a chokehold and knuckled the top of her head. Though she was gorgeous and sexy, Rosie was like a pal, permanently safe from any lecherous intentions, especially since she'd married Ethan.

"Hey," she gasped out, "no fair. I don't want to get messy again. I have a showing this afternoon."

Riley released her and got a sharp elbow to his middle. He grunted while Rosie quickly backed away. "Sucker," she said with a grin, then she turned and jogged toward the door.

Riley laughed. He did love Rosie, but he didn't want her. He didn't burn for her.

Not the way he did for Ms. Regina Foxworth.

REGINA KNEW it wasn't the wisest decision she'd ever made. And for a woman who prided herself on only making wise decisions, she should have been appalled at herself. She only had so much money for decorating her new house and putting in the alarm system that she'd promised Riley.

She tried to talk herself out of it, she really did. But as she stared at those big brown eyes, she fell madly in love. He was so cute with the way he laid his enormous ears back on his little round head, how he stared at her with bulging eyes, shivering with uncertainty. He probably wasn't the type of dog Riley had in mind, but the man said they were loyal pets, dedicated to their owners.

"I'll take him." Sometimes things just felt right. Like being a journalist. Like buying the house.

Like being near Riley.

This felt right, too. Now that she'd met this dog, no other would do, so she shelled out the six hundred dollars that she really couldn't spare. Love was love and it should never be denied. Not that she knew a lot about love. But she did know that she wanted it more than anything. And to get it, you had to give it, she reasoned. She could really love this dog.

While she carried him outside, he continued to shake and stare at her with those big, watchful eyes. She'd never seen such a pathetic look in her life. She wanted to crush him close, but he was so puny, she didn't dare. Gently, she stroked his skinny back and rubbed his soft neck.

She'd never felt a dog so soft. He had bunny fur, so cuddly and silky. And he didn't smell like a dog either. She rubbed her nose against his neck and got a tiny lick on the ear in return.

Once in the car, secured in the carrier, his teeny tiny mouth formed an O and he began to howl.

It was both hilarious, the way he looked, and heartwrenching the way he sounded. The mournful baying continued until Regina was in a near panic. "Shh. What's wrong?" Did he want her to hold him? "I have to drive, sweetie," she explained. "It wouldn't be safe. Soon as we get home, I'll cuddle you again, I promise."

At the sound of her voice, the dog quieted and inched to the edge of the small cage to sniff the air near her. His spindly little hind legs quivered and he continued to look sad, but trusting.

"Awww..." He was just so adorable. Big tears filled her eyes. She *had* made the right decision. Sticking one finger through the carrier, Regina rubbed behind his ear. "You're as soft as a baby bunny, did you know that?"

He cocked his head, listening to her, his ears still down in a woebegone display but he made no sounds of dismay.

"What should I name you?"

The ears came up. Regina marveled at his many expressions.

"How about...Elvis?" His ears pricked, then flattened again and he gave her a sideways look. "No? Then maybe Doe? You do look like a little deer, you know. Hmm. That doesn't appeal to you either? Something more manly then. I know. Butch. Or Butchie when you're being so adorable."

Soothed by her banter, he gave an excited yap of agreement and Regina nodded. "Butch it is."

For the rest of the ride home, Regina alternated her attention between her driving and the dog. She constantly scanned the road and surrounding area, still spooked from the time someone tried to run her off the berm. To calm herself and the dog, she spoke to him, being sure to use his name as the breeder suggested, so he could get used to it.

By the time they pulled into her apartment complex, he was looking around with interest, animated anytime she spoke to him. He continued to shake though.

People were coming and going, keeping the parking lot alive with a safe, surrounding crowd. Feeling secure again, she carried Butch, along with his paraphernalia, into her apartment. She'd bought bowls, food, chew sticks, a toothbrush, leash, collar and a cozy fleece-lined bed. She set Butch down first, watched him cower there on the floor, and decided he needed some encouragement.

Her apartment was small, only one bedroom, a bath, kitchenette and living area. "I'll be right back, Butch." She went to the kitchen to unload all the items, then came back for him. She found him sprinkling her couch.

"Oh, now that's just not right, Butch."

He slunk toward her, his head down in apology.

Regina's heart melted. "Honey, it's okay." She cuddled him close, got a tentative lick on her cheek. He was the most precious perfect dog, she decided, and carried him into the kitchen since that was where he'd spend most of his time. With a kiss to the top of his round head, she put him in his bed, then went back to clean her couch. When she returned to the kitchen, she found three more wet spots. Butch looked so very contrite, she couldn't hold it against him. She understood that he was nervous and needed reassurance. Instead of chastising him, she hugged and petted him some more, trying to let him know he was safe and secure and well loved.

By the time she had dinner going and Riley was due

to arrive, Butch had relaxed enough to play a little. He followed Regina everywhere she went, sometimes bounding here or there, sometimes turning excited circles. Charmed, Regina had to keep stopping to pick him up, kiss him and hug him.

Because she was on the second floor, she put a litter box on her small balcony for him to use and in no time he got the hang of going to the glass patio door to scratch. She used a short leash that kept him from reaching the edge of the balcony so he couldn't accidentally fall off and get hurt. He did his business like a trooper and came back in.

Of course, he marked his territory everywhere inside the apartment, too. Regina wasn't yet sure if he was uncertain of his boundaries, stubborn or just not very bright. She hoped the first, because the second and third didn't bode well for her peace of mind.

The chicken was done, the potatoes already mashed, when the knock sounded on her door. She recognized Riley's knock right off. Decisive, firm, just like the man himself.

Though she hated to admit it, she felt that familiar leap of her heart whenever he was near. They'd known each other three weeks now, and so far Riley had been attentive, courteous and understanding.

More important than that, he believed her somewhat wild stories about stalkers and threats when no one else would. Of course, Regina thought his belief just might be attributed to boredom. Riley used to be SWAT, for heaven's sake. He was used to excitement and danger.

In Chester, the most excitement he got was photographing old man Tilburn's house because the neighborhood rascals had toilet-papered it once again. For a man like Riley, a man of his skills and background, that had to add up to a lot of frustration. Even chasing Regina's ghosts had to be better than that.

But she wouldn't complain. Regardless of what motivated him, she needed his help, so she'd take what she could get.

She expected the thrill that skated through her when she started to open the door.

What she didn't anticipate was Butch going into a complete hostile frenzy. He transformed from tiny shivering dog into Tasmanian devil right before her eyes.

Riley called out, "Regina? It's me. Open up."

"Just a second." She picked up Butch, but holding the snarling, rigid, four-pound mass of meanness was nearly impossible. Outrage stiffened every muscle in his lean little body and he fought her to be free—so he could attack her visitor.

What a courageous dog!

Using one hand, Regina turned the locks on the door and then struggled to maintain her hold on Butch while Riley stepped inside. The dog broke free. Regina almost dropped him but managed to get him to the floor, head first.

He rolled, landed on his feet and like a shot, went after Riley.

Riley stood there, brows high, expression arrested, while Butch tried to tear his pant leg off. "What the hell? Is that a rabid squirrel?"

Indignant, Regina closed the door and crossed her arms. "Of course not. It's my dog, Butch."

"*That's* a dog?" Incredulity rang in his voice. "Are you sure?" His head tilted down at the wriggling fury hanging from his leg. "How can you tell?"

Offended on Butch's behalf, Regina huffed. She pulled the dog free and went about soothing him. "Shh. Butchie, it's okay. He's allowed in. Such a good dog. So brave."

Riley looked like he might puke. "That *is* a dog. What the hell is wrong with it?"

Regina sat on the couch. "Nothing. He's perfect."

"He can't weigh more than four pounds."

"He's four exactly." She rubbed Butch's belly and he rolled to his back, his skinny legs falling open, his eyes half-closed.

Riley pulled back. "Good God."

Regina didn't take him to task for that comment. After all, Butch was showing his equipment with no evidence of modesty whatsoever. She cleared her throat. "The breeder said I should have him neutered."

"He'll only weigh three pounds if you do." Grinning at his own joke, Riley took the seat beside her and reached out to pet the dog. Butch went berserk again, his doggy lips pulled back tight, rippling with menace, the whites of his eyes showing. One second he looked so innocent and sweet and the next he appeared like a vicious gnat.

"He needs time to get used to you," Regina explained in a rush, and hoped that was true. If Butch continued to act so contrary, what would she do?

In his usual calm manner, Riley surveyed Butch. "What kind of dog is it?"

"He's a pure bred Chihuahua. His beautiful coloring is very unique." She certainly thought him beautiful. "Red with black brindling."

Riley only nodded. "How much bigger will he get?"

"Oh, he's full-grown." She rubbed Butch's ears and watched his bulgy eyes narrow in bliss. "Isn't he just precious?"

"No." Riley frowned at her. "Please tell me this isn't your idea of a guard dog."

"But he's perfect," she said by way of answer. "You saw how he attacked you."

"And you saw how I held real still so I wouldn't accidentally hurt him."

She had noticed that. Riley was always so cautious with people, so careful. She knew a lot of that had to do with his training and his ability. It would be so easy for him to hurt someone, that he naturally tempered himself in almost all situations. Others might not be aware of his restraint, but Regina had seen it in his intense blue eyes, and she'd felt it during her lessons.

She'd also noticed that he hadn't been startled by Butch's attack. Most people would have jumped, maybe even screeched.

Not Riley. She couldn't imagine anything unsettling Riley enough to wring a screech out of him. With unparalleled calm, he'd taken in the situation and then reacted, without haste, careful not to hurt Butch.

Such an incredible guy.

Nodding, she said, "I did notice. Thank you."

Lounging back in his seat, Riley put one arm along

the couch back, almost touching her shoulder. Without leaving Regina's lap, Butch slanted a mean gaze his way, his rumbling growls a warning. Riley continued to watch the dog while speaking to Regina. "When do we eat? It smells good."

Flustered by the compliment, she came to her feet, holding Butch like an infant—which he seemed to enjoy. "It's ready now. We have to eat in the kitchen. I don't have a dining room. Once I get moved in I'll have a dining room, and we can use it then. I mean, if you're ever over for dinner at my new house...." Turning her back on Riley and rolling her eyes at her own rambling nonsense, she rushed into the kitchen. Hostesses should not ramble. They should feed their guests.

Riley followed. "Regina?"

"Hmm?" She turned after setting Butch in his bed. He came right back out of it, still watching Riley, inching closer for a sniff. Now that Regina no longer held him, he was jumpy enough to lurch back a step each time Riley moved.

"We'll be having plenty of dinners together."

The sneaky way the dog advanced distracted her. "We will?"

Butch was at Riley's foot now, his sniffing more purposeful. Knowing what Butch probably intended, Regina scrambled to find a chew stick. In no way did she want Butch to mark Riley. He was not part of the permanent territory and unlikely to become so.

Riley crouched down and held out a hand to Butch. The dog gave his fingers a thorough inspection, donned an angelic expression complete with big innocent eyes and a small doggy smile, and even allowed

Riley to rub under his chin. Teasing, Riley said, "You sure he wasn't bred with a rat?"

Regina, too, bent down to hand Butch the rawhide chew. The second she got near, Butch did an about-face. He snapped at Riley in warning, squirmed up close to Regina and accepted the chew.

"Contrary dog," Riley commented while standing up straight again.

Butch retreated to his bed to work over the chew. "He's getting used to you already."

Riley caught her hand and pulled her upright in front of him. Her heart pounded when his strong, warm fingers laced with hers, palm to palm.

"What about you, Red? You getting used to me, too?"

Oh boy, there was a load of innuendo in the way Riley said that. And truthfully, she was so used to him that when he wasn't around, she missed him. Dumb. Regina Foxworth did not allow herself fanciful infatuations. She thought to tell him that yes, she was used to him and why shouldn't she be? He was no different from any other man. But with his callused fingers holding hers, words stuck in her throat. She barely managed a shrug.

With his gaze holding her captive, his hand opened, slid slowly up her arm, over her shoulder and the side of her neck, along her jaw until his fingers curled around the back of her neck. Where he'd touched, gooseflesh sprang up and she trembled.

Softly, Riley whispered, "Wrong answer."

Her startled gasp emerged just as he urged her to her tiptoes. "Riley?"

"You need to accept a few things, Red."

She felt spellbound, uncertain. Anxious. But if she hesitated much longer, her chicken would burn and then she'd make a bad impression. She forced herself to say "Like?"

"Like this." He bent and kissed her.

2

THE TOUCH OF HIS MOUTH was brief, warm, firm. Regina barely had time to appreciate his taste before he lifted away the tiniest bit.

"Oh." Tentatively, thoughts of chicken obliterated, Regina laid her hands on his chest. He'd dressed in casual chinos and a polo shirt, but the domestic clothes couldn't hide the true nature of the man. The soft cotton fabric served an enticing contrast to the hard muscle, long bones and crisp hair underneath.

His eyes were more gray than blue now, glittering with heat. There was nothing even remotely domestic in the way he watched her. "More than anything," he rumbled low, "I'd like to carry you into your bedroom right now, strip you naked and make love all night." He closed his eyes a moment, drew a breath. When he looked at her again, some of that intense heat had been tempered. "But we've got a lot to get cleared up first."

Regina faltered. Make love all night? *Strip her naked?* They hadn't known each other *that* long. Regardless of her strong attraction to Riley, she wasn't the type of woman to leap into an affair. Responsible people utilized caution and thought before making that type of commitment.

Stepping back from him, she gestured to her tiny two-seater table. Her hand shook and she had to clear her throat twice before she could speak. "Sounds like we have a long talk ahead." Thankfully, her voice was only a little shaky. "Sit down while I serve dinner."

Riley watched her with indecision before silently agreeing. Regina could feel his gaze on her rump when she bent to pull the perfectly browned chicken out of the oven. Martha Stewart would be proud. Ms. Manners would applaud her.

As the delicious scents of stuffing and chicken wafted through the air, Butch perked up, his little nose raised and quivering with interest. Regina looked at him, but Riley said, "I wouldn't. Once you feed him table food, you'll never be able to stop. And it's not good for him anyway."

"Right." She knew that, and since she always tried to do the right thing, she hoped her dog would do the right thing as well. Giving Butch an apologetic shake of her head, she filled his bowl with dog food. Appeased, he began to eat while Regina carried the food to the table. The chicken was placed perfectly on a platter, the potatoes looked fluffy in a decorative bowl, and steam rose from the broccoli with melting butter atop it. She lit a scented candle in the middle of the table and everything was complete. Beautiful.

"What can I do to help?"

Regina stared at Riley, and he stared back, studying her. She'd expected him to sit and admire her dinner preparation skills, not watch her every move. But if he wanted to help...wasn't it a man's job to carve? She'd never had a man around long enough to know, and her father certainly hadn't been the type to worry about how food was cut. He was more a grab-and-stuff-it-in-your-mouth kind of guy.

Regina handed Riley the butcher knife and fork with a flourish. "Iced tea, milk?"

"Tea is fine." He stood to begin slicing apart the chicken. Regina noticed that he did an admirable job. He glanced up at her. "Why are you so nervous, Red?"

"I'm not."

"You are."

She sighed, unable to deny the obvious. "No more so than usual. That is, I'm always nervous." It was a complaint she often got from men. But now, with the man being Riley, she felt doubly unsettled. Add to that some unknown assailant who had tried to hurt her several times and might just try again, and to her way of thinking she had plenty of reason to be nervous.

"Because you're worried?"

"Yes." She poured the iced tea, sat, remembered she wanted music and popped back up. "I'll be right back." Seconds later, the stereo in her bedroom played low, adding soft sounds to the clink of china and silver.

Riley waited for her to return. He held her chair, but when she sat, he didn't retreat. Instead he bent down and kissed the side of her neck. Oh Lord, she'd never get used to this spontaneous kissing of his. At Mach speed, he'd taken them from acquaintances, maybe friends, to something much more intimate.

Fighting the urge to gasp again, she stiffened. Where he'd pressed his mouth, her neck tingled and felt damp. A strange but pleasant warmth rippled through her.

Riley spoke softly into her ear, adding to her awareness. "You need to be comfortable being alone with me, Red."

The way he said that, all seductive and low, made her stomach flip-flop. "I do?" At this rate, she'd never be able to eat. It'd look like she didn't appreciate her own culinary skills.

"Yeah." He brushed her nape with the back of one finger, then circled the table and sat in his chair, facing her, casual as you please, as if he hadn't just been teasing her, turning her on.

"Um…why?"

He picked up his fork. "Starting today, we're going to be alone together." His gaze caught and held hers. "A lot."

THE FOOD WAS DELICIOUS. He'd had no idea that Regina was such a fine cook. For long moments, they ate in silence. He waited to see what Regina would say to his statement, but she just sat there, watching him cautiously, occasionally nibbling on her food.

He didn't want to spoil her dinner, so he sat back and studied her. "I guess you want me to explain?"

She cleared her throat. "That'd be nice, yes."

A starched linen napkin had been placed beside his plate. Since it was there, Riley used it to pat his mouth. "All right. You're not showing much improvement at the gym."

Her shoulders sank the tiniest bit. Riley wasn't sure if it was disappointment or relief. "I know. I'm not a very physical person."

He intended to hold all judgments on that until he had her in bed. Then he'd see just how physical he could coax her into being. "You don't need physical strength, Regina. But you do have to stop worrying about other people watching you."

She winced. "I know. It's just that I hate looking like a fool."

"Once you know what you're doing, you'll look like a pro."

"Yes, of course," she quickly agreed. "I'll try harder, I promise."

He didn't believe that for a minute. "Regina?"

She glanced up at him, her brows raised quizzically.

"I'm going to give you very private lessons from now on. Just the two of us." He looked at her mouth. "All alone. No spectators."

She stared at him for three seconds. "You are?"

Riley nodded, a little put out that she questioned every damn thing he said, like she couldn't believe it or doubted it to be true. He wasn't a liar, damn it.

Stunned by that mental statement, he shook his head and made a quick amendment: he wouldn't lie to *her*, and not about this. Other lies, lies from his past, were well buried.

Holding on to his patience, Riley continued his explanation. "There's not much room here at your place, so we can't really get going tonight."

Her mouth opened. In anticipation, shock or horror? Riley couldn't quite tell. "You can either come to my place, or the gym after hours."

She held perfectly still. Tonight she had her thick hair twisted at the back of her head and held in place with a fancy gold clip. It had been somewhat loosened by the kiss he'd given her earlier. The florescent overhead lights brought out the deeper reds and lighter golds, mixed in with the auburn. It also reflected the wariness in her green eyes.

She wore a freshly pressed sleeveless green V-neck shirt and low-riding cotton slacks. Her sandals showed off her meticulous pedicure.

From the top of her head to the tips of her toes, she was polished to a shine. She'd even managed to do dinner with no additional mess, putting things away as she used them so that no empty pans sat on the stove and no seasonings were out.

Riley wanted to see her mussed.

He wanted to see her sweat.

He wanted to hear Ms. Suzy Homemaker crying out in raw sexual excitement without a single thought as to how she looked, concerned only with the deep, driving pleasure.

Damn, he had to stop that train of thought or he'd be seducing her right now.

Finally, she nodded. "Thank you." Her voice sounded a little raspy. "It does embarrass me. I think it'll be easier without others watching. But, Riley, mostly it's you that I worry about."

"Me?" Sipping his iced tea, he watched her, thinking it wasn't such a bad thing if he unsettled her. It meant she held at least a small amount of awareness for him as a man.

She pleated her napkin. She straightened her fork. Suddenly she blurted, "Are you attracted to me?"

"Yes."

She seemed surprised by his immediate answer.

Then she chewed on her lips. "I'm attracted to you, too."

She made that admission with the same regret she might have given a murder confession.

"I know." He hadn't known. He'd hoped. He was pretty sure. But he'd wanted confirmation.

Now he had it.

"It...bothers me, the idea of you seeing me all messy and sweaty."

Hearing her say it sharpened his desire. "Eventually, I'll see you every way there is." He toyed with his iced tea glass, his gaze never wavering from hers. "When we have sex, you'll definitely be sweaty. Messy, too. That's the way it is with good sex. But I'm willing to bet you'll look hot as hell."

Her breathing deepened and her brows puckered in thought. After a long hesitation, she said, "You, um, you treat Rosie like a pal."

"Rosie is a pal."

"But she's also a very attractive woman."

Leaning back in his seat, Riley nodded. "Agreed."

"And yet you never have romantic thoughts about her because she's become your pal."

Riley had no idea where she was going with this. Women could be so confusing, even to a man who prided himself on getting past the surface stuff. Oh, he could detect some of her thoughts. She was uncertain, interested, wary. But he wanted to know *why* she felt so uncertain.

He eyed her, then decided a little truth couldn't hurt the situation. "Who says?"

Confusion left her face blank. "Who says... Well, Rosie said. She assured me that she loved Ethan and—"

"She does." It had recently become very clear that Rosie had always loved Ethan—she'd just been waiting around for him to come to his senses and realize that he loved her, too.

"—and that Ethan was a good friend of yours."

"He is." With Harris and Buck, they made a regular foursome, but he and Ethan had more in common. They were all friends, but if Riley ever had his back to the wall, he'd trust Ethan more than any other man.

"Then—"

"You think because we're friends, I shouldn't have sexual thoughts about her?" He stretched out his long legs beneath the table and bumped into her small feet. "You and I are friends, and I have plenty of sexual thoughts about you."

Her eyes widened comically. "Plenty?"

It was his turn to smile. "All day, every day, as a matter of fact."

She stewed on that for a bit before speaking again. "But see, that's just it. I thought you felt about me the way you feel about Rosie, except you're closer with her."

"Not a chance."

"You're not close to her?"

"Very close. But the way I feel about you is on the other end of the scale. I don't intend to ever sleep with Rosie." He let his gaze drop to her breasts. "You, however, I intend to get naked with just as soon as it can be arranged."

Her eyes dilated in shock, but he also saw reciprocal

interest in the way her breathing deepened and how her skin warmed. Despite all that, she shook her head. "You should probably know, Riley, I don't sleep around."

"You're a virgin?"

More color stained her cheeks and she frowned. "No, I didn't say that." Then she added in a mumble, "For heaven's sake, I'm twenty-eight years old."

"So you're saying you don't want to sleep with me?" He knew damn good and well that wasn't true. But would she be honest?

"Of course I do."

He grinned.

"I mean, I do, but I'm not going to. Not anytime soon, that is. We barely know each other."

He'd known her long enough to understand exactly how he felt. "We've known each other better than three weeks now. That's not exactly a sneeze. And because of the lessons, we've been physically close."

"You're keeping count?"

She was clearly astonished by that. Hell, it still stunned Riley a little, the depth of what he felt. But he didn't want her panicking on him, so he backed off. "Let's finish eating, then we'll talk about it more. By the way, you're a hell of a cook. I'm impressed."

Relieved by the change of topic, she nodded. "I wanted you to be. Impressed, I mean." She caught herself and her gaze jerked up to his. "That is, I try to impress everyone."

"Yeah? Why is that, Red? You don't think just being yourself is good enough?" There was so much he still had to learn about her. Funny how appearances meant nothing to him because they weren't something you could trust. Yet, they meant the world to her.

The contrast in their views might have discouraged him, but he figured he was at least making headway now.

"Maybe." She propped her head on her hand, realized that wasn't the proper way to sit and jerked upright again. "Actually I've thought about this a lot, about why I'm the way I am. Every so often, I wish I could be different because sometimes it has the opposite effect and just drives people nuts."

"What people?"

"Co-workers, friends. Men."

He didn't give a damn what other men thought of her. If they steered clear, hell, he was glad. "Rosie and Ethan and Buck and Harris like you fine." He smiled. "I like you more than fine. But I am curious why you're so worried about what other people think. That is, if you care to talk about it."

She pleated and fussed with her napkin. "It's silly really. Maybe something of a habit left over from when I was young."

"You were a fussy child?"

His teasing put a self-conscious half smile on her face. "Yes. Very fussy, I guess. See, I came from a...a dirty farmhouse." She wrinkled her nose with that confession. "And when I say dirty, I'm not exaggerating. It's awful to admit, but we lived like pigs."

Not sure that he understood, Riley asked, "You were poor?"

"Poor and slovenly are not the same thing, but yes, we were poor, too. I've never been certain if it was necessary, if they just couldn't make enough money or if they simply mismanaged what they made." She shrugged. "My parents sustained us from paycheck to paycheck. If we ran out in the middle of the week, or something came up—as things always do—they'd borrow or beg."

The expression on her face twisted his heart. Softly, he said, "That had to be rough."

"I hated it and it embarrassed me."

The emotional plethora took Riley off guard. Being a private man, he couldn't imagine discussing so much of his personal background. "So you've worked to change your life. There's nothing wrong with that."

"It was never my life." She sipped her tea, scooted her broccoli around on her plate with the edge of her fork. "It was my mother's, my father's and my younger brother's. But not mine."

No, Riley couldn't quite imagine her ever being comfortable in those circumstances. She was so prim, proper and precise now, that it must have been almost painful for her.

"You didn't accept the circumstances of your youth."

"For as far back as I can remember, even as a young kid, I tried to make it different. Everything I owned was old and stained, but I did my best to always keep it clean and pressed." She glanced up at him and gave a low laugh. "My brother used to make fun of me for being so meticulous. The other kids we knew.... They liked to call us names and poke fun at us."

Riley hated that anyone had hurt her feelings, even though it had happened long ago. And her brother... It was ridiculous to be angry at him when he'd been no more than a boy, too. But that didn't change how Riley felt. "Kids can be pretty cruel when no one is teaching them better."

"Maybe. But if you'd ever seen our farm or car or how my parents behaved in public, you'd understand why the kids treated us the way they did. I understood it. And I knew my family would never change. After I graduated high school, I moved away, got a job as an errand girl with a small paper and worked my way up to reporter."

Riley smiled. Reporter was a bit of a stretch considering the small pieces she wrote. Then again, her human-interest stories for the local paper were always entertaining. She'd done a stellar article on Ethan that had made the fire department, as well as the whole town, proud.

Riley thought about it and decided selective sharing was good. It forged a bond that would bring them closer together, and that was his ultimate goal. There were parts of himself he could discuss, parts that weren't buried deep and that wouldn't reveal anything beyond the surface.

He mentally skimmed a variety of topics and settled on his safest bet—family. "My mother isn't immaculate or anything."

Her interest obvious, she glanced up at him with a smile. "No?"

"She keeps the place tidy, but it's always well lived in. I have two younger brothers, one older."

"Four boys? My goodness."

"Yeah, Mom felt the same way." He laughed. "The

others still live near to home and they drop in a lot with their broods. Between the three of them, I have ten nieces and nephews."

"Wow. A big family."

He acknowledged that with a shrug. "Mom is old-fashioned, the type who wants to feed you the minute you show up and fusses around you the whole time you're there. I haven't been home to see her in a while." That was something he should remedy, Riley decided. Funny that he hadn't much considered how long it had been until Regina started discussing her family.

Wondering how Regina would react to the casual mess around his mother's house, he pushed his plate away. "Maybe next time I go, you could come along with me."

Her eyes shot wide. "You want me to meet your mother?"

She sounded as if he'd asked her to swim with sharks. "And Dad, too. You'd like them."

She had nothing to say to that so Riley pressed her. "What about your folks? Do you visit with them at all?" He wouldn't really be surprised if she'd broken all ties, but it'd be a shame. When all was said and done, family should be there for you, and vice versa.

"They're gone now." There was a wistful, sad note to her voice. "Mom died years ago from cancer and Dad passed away from a stroke two years after. The farm was sold and my brother and I split the profits. That's how I bought my house. I've been sitting on that money for a while."

Riley had wondered about that. He didn't imagine a small-town reporter earned much income. "I'm sorry."

"It was a long time ago. I loved them, but I was never very close with them. We had a...strained relationship." She hesitated, and Riley wondered if she'd pull back now, if she'd return to being evasive. Instead, she shrugged. "They thought I was snooty."

With almost no prodding at all, she continued to open up to him. In his experience, reporters pried into anyone and everyone's life, but clammed up when it came to their own personal issues. He couldn't help wondering if her openness was a compliment reserved for special people. Did she feel safer with him? Did she trust him?

"Snooty, huh?" He pretended to study her head to toe, then nodded. "Circumspect, yes. Meticulous, maybe. But not snooty."

"Thank you." She tucked in her chin to hide her smile. "My brother still accuses me of thinking I'm better than them."

"Do you?"

"Think I'm better? No. But I'm certainly wiser about how I handle my life." Her long look seemed like a warning, one he fully intended to ignore. He would have her, and soon. "My parents had a great farm that they let go to ruin because they refused to do any real work. It should have been worth five times as much, but they'd never taken care of it. The house was so run-down it had to be demolished. There wasn't a piece of furniture or a dish to be salvaged."

"No mementos at all?"

"A few photographs that my brother and I split. My

folks didn't believe in cherishing the past or planning for the future. They had the barest medical coverage and of course, it wasn't enough. Now my brother seems just like them. He flits from one job to the next, one woman to another."

Sounded like a lot of guys Riley knew, men who wouldn't grow up and so, at least in his opinion, weren't really men.

"He's already spent his inheritance and doesn't have a thing to show for it. I asked what he intended to do when he retired, but he just laughs and says he has a lifetime to worry about it. He hasn't learned at all."

"But you have?"

"Absolutely." She met his gaze squarely. "The house is an investment in my future, but I have others as well. If I get sick, I'll be able to take care of myself, not rely on others or end up in the care of the state. I'm careful about everything I do and I don't give in to impulses."

Impulses like sexual desire? Did she hope to deny the chemistry between them? Riley didn't correct her but he knew different. He could be persuasive and he never gave up easily.

At his long silence, her chin lifted. "What about you?"

"What about me?"

She looked self-conscious but forged on. "Do you have a retirement plan? And you mentioned your place. Do you have your own house or are you renting?"

The inquisition so surprised him, Riley laughed. "Tell me, Red, are you curious for personal reasons, sizing me up as husband material, or are you mentally working on that damn article?"

She stiffened, but she didn't lie. "A little of each maybe, though it's certainly too early to be thinking about anything serious between us."

"You really think so?"

Her face went blank, then pink with confusion. She forged on. "And I wouldn't write the article without your permission. It's just that the whole community hero angle worked so well with Ethan, I know people would eat up a life story on you."

He ignored that because his life wasn't anybody's business. "But you're personally interested, right?"

She chewed on her lips again. "We're not involved, Riley, so it's more curiosity than anything."

"I want to be involved."

She pressed back in her chair. She blinked, studied his face, then looked down at her hands. "You know, Riley, it occurs to me that this could get pretty muddled."

"How so?" Riley felt strangely sated. He'd had a delicious meal, cozy conversation and the sight of Regina seated across from him. It was the kind of setting he could get used to—the kind of setting he · hadn't wanted again until he'd met her.

He knew exactly how he'd like to end the day, but after everything she'd confessed, he had his doubts about her cooperation. He could be patient, especially since all indications led him to believe he'd eventually win.

"You say you believe me about the attacks."

"I do."

"Then don't you think we should keep the personal and the professional separate? Won't it be hard for you to be objective if we're...well, sleeping with each other?"

Objectivity had flown out the window within hours of meeting her. He drank the last of his iced tea and nodded at her plate. "What I think is that you should eat some of this great dinner you fixed."

"I am eating." She took two more bites, then went on in a rush. "Why would you believe me when no one else does?"

"It's easy enough to understand. You finish eating and I'll tell you a story, okay?"

"All right."

She still only picked at her food, but he felt better knowing he hadn't completely ruined her meal. "Back when I was a new evidence tech, before I became SWAT, I got called to the scene where a guy had broken into his seventeen-year-old girlfriend's house. The mother had forbid the girl to see him anymore, but when she left to go shopping, he snuck over. When the girl tried to send him away, he got unreasonably furious, choking her and banging her head on the wall a few times."

Regina's head came up, a broccoli floret dangling from her fork. "Dear God."

"The mom got home in time to pull him off her," Riley assured her, but as usual, the bitter memories filled him with anger. Too many times, he hadn't been able to make a difference. "The detectives got there just before me, but the boyfriend had already fled. They were speaking with the mom and daughter, and the dad who had just arrived home. Patrol tells me that the mom wants to prosecute the guy, but the daughter doesn't. When I explain that her boyfriend committed a Felony One—aggravated burglary—which carries the same sentence as murder, the mom starts backing up, too."

"But her daughter…"

"Has purpling choke marks on her neck and bruises on her cheek and temple. Still, she just kept saying, 'But I love him. He didn't mean to hurt me.'"

Regina threw down her fork. "Well, what in the world did he think would happen when he manhandled her that way?"

"Men like that don't concern themselves with the victim. And with the daughter spouting all the classic I-have-no-self-esteem phrases that you get from abused women, there wasn't much we could do. The dad was noticeably silent, only occasionally saying, 'I think I just need to have a talk with the boy.'"

"Unbelievable."

"No, honey, unfortunately it's all too believable and cops run into that crap every day. We had to leave with no charges filed because the victims wouldn't prosecute. I was pissed, the other detective was scratching his head and then the female officer says, "I can tell you what's going on in there. Dad's beaten Mom up a few times and the daughter knows it. Mom doesn't want to say anything because she might get another beating and the poor girl thinks this is normal behavior because she's lived with it for years."

Riley's hands fisted on the tabletop. He wouldn't tell

Regina that eventually the girl had run off with the jerk—and died because of it.

Subdued, Regina left her seat and came around to Riley's side. Immediately, Butch did the same. He ran from his bed, stretched up with his paws on her thigh and begged to be held. Regina scooped him up close, rubbing her nose against his soft fur but speaking to Riley. "I'm sorry."

Riley gave her a one-arm hug, pulling her into his side. Because he was still sitting, his face was level with the subtle swell of her breasts. Well, her breasts and a fuzzed-up, irritable Butch who didn't want Riley to touch her.

The dog was too territorial, but Riley understood how he felt. "Yeah, me, too." He forced his gaze to her face. "But you know what, Red? It taught me something. There are all kinds of perspectives and things we never see. And women, God bless them, are pretty damned intuitive. If you say someone is after you, I'd be an idiot not to take you seriously. And, believe me, I'm not an idiot."

She gave a small, tremulous smile. "Thank you. It... Well, it feels better, safer, just knowing someone isn't writing me off as a nut."

Riley pushed back his chair and came to his feet. Oh yeah, he knew exactly how Butch felt because the urge to hold her was nearly overwhelming. "Tell you what, Red. Let's put the dishes away, then go to the living room and you can tell me everything that's been going on."

"Everything?"

"From the beginning. Maybe we'll be able to sort

things out." He put his hand at the small of her back and urged her away from the table. "Do you think Killer can entertain himself a few minutes?"

The dog managed a sideways glare and a roll of his lip, but when Regina put him in his bed, this time he circled, dug at the bedding for a few seconds, then plopped down to sleep with his nose noticeably close to his rump.

Her kitchen was so immaculate, it didn't take any time at all to put things away. The leftovers went into matching containers in the fridge. The dishes were rinsed and put in uniform order in the dishwasher. Regina was so orderly, so clean, it unnerved Riley a bit.

Would she expect everyone to be that tidy? Curious as to how judgmental she might be, Riley said, "You've been to Rosie's place before, right?"

"Yes, why?"

"How'd you like it?" Rosie was tidy, but nowhere near as big a neat freak as Regina.

She thought about it for a moment, then smiled. "From the first time I stepped into Rosie's house, it felt cozy, like a home." She gave a soft laugh that sank into him. "But Rosie's that way. Very warm and open and friendly. I like her a lot."

Satisfied by her answer, Riley smiled. "Yeah, me, too."

Together they washed the pans, Regina cleaning and Riley drying. Damn, but he had a good time doing it. Just being with her calmed something turbulent inside him, making him feel more at peace with himself and his life. But slowly the serenity of the moment expanded into heightened awareness. He wanted her, and not having her was torture.

When her hands were completely submersed in soapy water, Riley moved behind her. Holding her waist so she couldn't slip away, he deliberately pressed in, relishing the feel of her full bottom against his groin. A short groan rumbled in his chest.

One day soon, after she'd accepted him, he'd take her this way, from behind, sinking deep, feeling her buttocks on his abdomen and thighs. He'd be able to cover her breasts with his hands, toy with her stiffened nipples, slip his fingers down her belly to her...

"Riley?"

He ignored the hardening of his body, the surge of lust, to nibble carefully on her ear. Without intentional thought, he further aroused her, letting his breath tickle her ear, using the edge of his tongue to tantalize the sensitive nerve endings along the tendons in her neck. "You don't want to sleep with me yet, Red, but you will soon. In the meantime, a little kissing won't hurt anything, right?" Before she could answer, he dipped his tongue into her ear, then gently sucked her earlobe. His accelerated breaths fanned the delicate, baby-fine hairs at her temple.

"No." Her hands went still, just dangling over the edge of the sink, not quite in the water, not quite out. She tipped her head back to his shoulder and closed her eyes.

Riley leaned around her to see her face. "No what, honey?" He pressed one hand from her waist to her belly, spreading his fingers wide in masculine possession. His thumb dipped into her navel through her clothes, pressing gently, symbolic of so much more. Few people understood the erogenous zones of a woman's body, how small touches, when combined just right, could elicit carnal reactions.

In his training, he'd learned a lot about pressure points that could cripple, but the reverse was also true. He knew the places where exquisite, almost unbearable pleasure existed.

He could make her come, right here, right now, without undue effort, and that knowledge had his entire body straining in need. But he didn't want to push her. The constraint cost him, making him tremble and turning his voice hoarse. "No, you don't want me to do this, or no, there's nothing wrong with it?"

"There's nothing wrong with it."

A shudder rippled through him; she'd seemed so wary of sexual involvement with him that any capitulation now felt like a major triumph.

Suddenly she turned and plastered herself up against him, breasts to abdomen, belly to groin. "I want to kiss you, Riley. I just don't want you to expect it to lead to bed."

"All right."

Her green eyes narrowed with mingled surprise and uncertainty. "All right, what?"

He settled his hands on her hips, urging her closer still, so he could feel the rounded, feminine contours of her body. "All right, you can kiss me. Go ahead."

"Oh." She looked at his mouth, licked her own, and Riley nearly lost it.

"Hurry up, Red."

"Okay then." With her soapy hands sliding around

his neck, she went on tiptoe and her mouth touched his.

Riley waited, his heart thundering, his erection straining, his testicles tight. With ruthless determination, he gathered his control around him and kept his stance relaxed, his expression calm, when in reality his emotions bordered on savage. He'd never wanted any woman the way he wanted Regina.

Her warm velvet tongue licked out again, this time over his lips. "Riley?"

"Yeah?"

"Open your mouth for me."

That did it. As carefully as he could manage considering the tumultuous raging of his libido, Riley gathered her fully against him. With her heartbeat echoing his, he opened his mouth but didn't let her take the lead. His tongue slid in, deep and slow, mating with hers, teasing, showing her with his mouth how he wanted to take her with his body. Their hot breaths mingled, their hands clutched. Her body relaxed and sighed into his, so soft and fluid and feminine; his grew more taut with pounding lust.

He'd promised himself only a few kisses when he started this, but then he hadn't counted on the effect of her full and enthusiastic involvement. Before he'd even had time to think it through, he had a small breast in one hand, a firm, lush cheek in the other.

Their groans sounded at the same time.

Her nipple stiffened against his palm, a plea that he couldn't ignore. Using only his open palm, Riley brushed his hand over her again and again, abrading her nipples, giving her only so much. Her fingers tightened in his hair. She pulled her mouth away to gulp for air. "Riley?"

She said his name as an invitation, an appeal for more. "Regina..."

The sudden furious yapping of the dog startled them both. As if he'd only just then realized their physical closeness, Butch ran wild circles around them, snapping at Riley's leg without actually touching, making his discontent with the situation well known.

It hit Riley that his control had definitely slipped. For that brief moment, he'd lost all sense of himself, acting solely on need. It was an awesome, almost frightening admission. No one, not even his wife, and not even the worst imaginable scene, had so much as caused a flicker of loss in his innate control. He'd considered it an unchangeable part of him, like his height and bone structure.

One glance at Regina's hot face and he wanted to curse. "I'm sorry."

She shook her head. "No. No reason to apologize." She smoothed her hands down the front of her blouse, realized they were wet and tucked them behind her. Her smile was entirely false and self-conscious. "Would you like coffee?"

Strangely insulted, Riley stared at her. They'd shared a killer kiss, he'd had his hands all over her, and she wanted to continue playing proper hostess. "What I'd like," he muttered under his breath, "is to finish what we started."

"Excuse me?"

"Nothing." He needed a distraction and fast. The obvious distraction was now chewing on his heel while growling like a banshee. Riley reached down for Butch, but with his expression so dark the dog tucked in his tail and scurried away with due haste. Issuing a grievous sigh, Riley caught Butch with one hand and held him up close. Regina stood next to him like a fretful mother while the dog tried to brazen it out, grumbling, snarling and looking to Regina for rescue.

"Shh," Riley soothed while stroking the narrow back with one finger. The dog was smaller than his foot, his legs no thicker than Riley's baby finger and he fit fully into one hand. Butch quieted just a bit, giving Riley a suspicious look reminiscent of Regina's. "Good boy. See, I'm not so evil, huh? I saw that you weren't actually biting me, just trying to scare me off. You don't trust me with Regina. But you're going to have to get used to me touching her, buddy, because I intend to touch her a lot."

Regina said, "You do?"

Riley slanted her a look. "Since we're done here, let's go into the living room. The sooner I can figure out what the hell's going on with your attacker, the sooner we can get beyond it."

Regina dried her hands, neatly folded the dish towel to hang over the bar and hurried after him. "And then what?"

"And then I can concentrate on just you." He smiled at her over his shoulder, a deliberate smile, hot and suggestive. She stopped dead in her tracks, blinked twice, then followed him into the room.

And damned if she didn't wear a coy little smile of her own.

3

"IT STARTED after my assignment in the park."

The second Regina sat beside him, Butch snapped at Riley again and jumped over into her lap. Traitorous dog. "What park? Around here?"

"No, where I used to work before moving to Chester." While she spoke, she absently petted the dog and within minutes Butch was sound asleep again. "It was a new park opening. There'd been a lot of problems with it because some of the bigger businesses wanted to use the area for a parking lot. The arguments were pretty good on both sides: beautify the land with a park to draw visitors to the area, or use it to provide adequate parking so people would come to the stores to shop, thereby actually spending money."

"So I guess the park won?"

She nodded. "It was in the news every day. City hall got more action than it'd seen in months. The mayor had started to look pretty harried before everything got settled. The paper I worked for ran regular articles about it, then they sent me there to get photos and to do a write-up a week before the park officially opened. It was my biggest feature, a two-page spread."

Riley smiled at her enthusiasm. Sitting so close to her, seeing her so animated, made it impossible not to touch her. He reached toward her, and Butch came off her lap like a whirlwind. Riley didn't duck away. He held his hand out while Butch pretended to bite. He came close, but never actually closed his teeth on Riley.

"Just like I thought. All bluster." He kept his tone soft so he wouldn't upset the dog more. "You're ferociously defensive, aren't you, squirt? I like that." And then, despite Butch's complaints, he rubbed his ears. Butch gave up and enjoyed the attention. "So what happened at the park?"

"Everything was going well at first. I took some pictures of the elaborate fountain, the new swing sets, the pond with ducks and geese. It really is a beautiful spot." She glanced down at Butch and blushed. "I even got to meet my favorite politician."

"Yeah? And who's that?"

"Senator Welling. He was there with an intern, doing the same thing I was doing, checking out the park. He'd supported it, you see. He always supports the conservation of land whenever possible. I've admired him so long, I even took a few pictures of him. He waved to the camera for me."

Riley sighed. For a reporter, she sure had a hard time getting around to the point. "So what happened, Red? Did someone attack you in the park? Did the good senator try to come on to you—"

"No! Senator Welling isn't like that." She looked genuinely annoyed by his teasing remarks. "The reason I admire him so much is because he's such a dedicated family man. He's a wonderful politician, too, of course, and I agree with most of his political stands, but it's his dedication to his wife and children that's his real appeal."

Personally, Riley thought the man was a schmooze, but then he wasn't about to get into a political debate with Regina. "I'll take your word for it."

Still disgruntled, she said, "He politely posed for my pictures, even did one with him and the intern standing on either side of the fountain. He walked me to my car *and* opened my car door for me."

Maybe he'd been coming on to her after all and Regina was just too naive to realize it. "So what happened at the park that made you feel threatened?"

"Oh, it was as I was leaving the park. I was almost to the main road when some jerk sideswiped me."

Riley straightened. "What do you mean, he sideswiped you?"

"I drive a little silver Escort, and this fancy SUV tried to pass me, but he didn't clear my hood before cutting back into my lane. His rear end hit my front bumper and my car went into a spin, then off the road. I plowed into a tree. The guy didn't even stop, just kept going."

"And you think that's related somehow to—"

"If you'll just let me finish," she said in exasperation.

"Sorry." Riley held up both hands. "By all means." He only hoped she got to the point before midnight.

"It wasn't easy, but I got the car out of the ditch and made it pretty close to the main road. I probably did even more harm to the car, but I didn't like the idea of sitting there alone in the park, especially since it was starting to get dark."

"Smart."

"I thought so. My cell phone had gone dead, so I thought I'd have a long walk ahead of me, but then the senator came by and he drove me to a phone. He even offered to wait with me, but I told him to go on. Wasn't that awfully nice of him?"

"He's supposed to serve the people, honey."

"Not as a taxi. Anyway, I called my boss from a diner. He called for a tow truck then came to pick me up and drive me back to my car. You won't believe what I found."

Numerous possibilities ran through his mind, but he said only, "What?"

"Someone had broken into it."

"You didn't lock it up?"

"Of course I did. But the driver's side window was smashed. I thought for sure my stereo, speakers and CDs would be gone."

"I gather they weren't?"

"No. The car had been ransacked, my glove box emptied, all my papers strewn around, but nothing was missing as far as I could tell."

Riley frowned. He had to admit that sounded odd. Had someone been looking for something specific? "What did the police say about it?"

"That I must have returned in time to scare the robbers off."

Possibly. But he wasn't one to always accept the most obvious explanation. "You have another theory?"

"Yes. Looking back, I think that SUV ran me off the road on purpose. I think he came back later to look for something in my car."

"If that's so, if he was really that determined, why not just follow you home?" Even saying it made Riley's protective instincts twitch. If someone *had* followed her, what might have happened? He didn't even want to contemplate such a scenario. From now on, he intended to keep a closer watch on her.

"I'm not a criminal so I can't know how a criminal's mind works. But maybe he knew I lived in a busy complex, so going through my car wouldn't have been easy. The thing is, I can't imagine what I'd have that anyone would want, but I am really grateful that Senator Welling was there to drive me into town. If he hadn't..."

"You might have been sitting in your car, all alone, when the burglar showed up." Riley reached out and took her hand. "Could be your presence would have deterred him."

"But maybe not. He did run me off the road without much concern, so maybe he'd have just hit me over the head or something. Maybe he'd have even—"

Riley's teeth hurt from clenching his jaw. "Don't." No way in hell did he want her to cavalierly discuss deadly possibilities. They'd already occurred to him, of course, so he didn't need embellishment of his own grisly thoughts.

"Well, after everything else that's happened..."

"Such as?"

"I left work one night after finishing up some research. Phone calls mostly. It was about eight, dark outside already. Just as I started to step off the curb, a black Porsche nearly ran me down. I had to jump back fast to keep from being hit. I landed on the ground, tore my panty hose, broke two fingernails and twisted my ankle."

Anger swelled inside him. "Jesus. You could have been killed."

"I think that was the point. But the police wrote it off as a sloppy driver, not a deliberate intent to hit me. They thought it was unrelated to the other incident and they said there was nothing they could do about it since I didn't get the license plate number."

Rationally, Riley knew they were right. Without a direct witness or a way to track down the car, the police were helpless. But at the very least, they could have taken the threat to her seriously.

Only, he didn't know if he would have either. Not with so little to go on. The first violation appeared to be a bungled burglary. The second *could* have been a drunk driver or a speeding kid....

"A week after that, some bully tried to grab my purse. I held on to it—"

Riley had gotten more and more rigid as the enormity of her dilemma sank in, and now his control nearly snapped. *"You held on?"*

The dog lunged at him for raising his voice. Riley pulled Butch up to his chest with one hand cradled under his body. He bounced him as he'd often done with his nieces and nephews when they were fussy babies. Butch had no idea what to make of it. He looked confused, but he quieted. His eyes were wide, his ear perked up. He peered at Regina, then back at Riley.

"It was *my* purse, Riley. No way was I going to just give it up."

"He could have hurt you, damn it."

"He *did* hurt me."

Through stiff lips, Riley growled, "Tell me."

His tone was so gruff, she gave him an uncertain look. "He...well, he belted me. Gave me a black eye."

"*Son of a bitch.*"

"Riley!"

The dog howled and Riley released Regina's hand to stroke the dog's back, scratch his ears. "What did the police have to say about that?"

In a strange shift of mood, Regina scooted closer to him and stroked his shoulder. "It was weeks ago, Riley. There's no reason to get so upset now."

She attempted to soothe him much as Riley soothed the fractious dog. "I'm furious, not upset," Riley muttered, then added, "Women get upset."

"Your shoulders are all bunched and one eye is narrowed more than the other and you've got this strange tick in your jaw."

"Fury."

"All right, then don't get so furious. That won't help."

Knowing she was right, he drew a deep breath that didn't abate his anger one bit but gave him the elusion of calm. "Tell me what the cops said."

"Well, they were a little more concerned this time because after the guy hit me, my purse was dumped, only he didn't steal anything. My wallet was right there with two credit cards and about forty dollars, but he just rifled through the stuff on the ground, cursed me, and when we heard people coming, he ran off without a single thing."

Butch flopped onto his back in Riley's arms and went back to sleep. Apparently, he liked the rough rocking.

"What did the man look like?"

"I'm not sure. It was raining that day so he had on a slicker that closed up to his throat. He wore a hat and sunglasses, though there wasn't a speck of sunshine to be found. I noticed he was dark because he had five o'clock shadow and dark sideburns. His hands were tanned."

"Did the police try to follow him?"

"By the time they got there, he was long gone. They didn't know what to think until I explained about the other things that had happened. Then they wanted me to tell them about all my recent assignments." She shrugged. "But there hasn't been anything that would upset anyone. I don't write derogatory, cutting-edge pieces." She looked disgruntled with that admission. "I cover parks and new cookbooks and special-interest groups."

"So what had you written?" Riley continued rocking the dog. Butch twisted awkwardly, tucking the back of his head into Riley's neck and nuzzling closer in doggy bliss. Damn it, he was starting to like the dog.

"Let's see. I'd done the park feature...."

"No, before that. Everything started the day of the park, right? So it had to be something you'd done prior to that."

"That makes sense." She scrunched up her nose in thought. "Well, I did do an article on a professional football player arrested for a DUI, but my angle was on the time he donated to underprivileged children, something he'd been doing even before being assigned community service. And I did an interview with the author of a popular cookbook. The book was a hit, but it turned out the author had stolen some of the recipes from her mother-in-law's great-great-grandmother. But she in turn donated half her royalties to her mother-in-law's favorite charity, and they worked everything out amicably."

Riley frowned in thought. "Not exactly life-altering news, huh?"

Sounding defensive, Regina said, "I have done a few more critical pieces."

"Like?"

"About a month earlier I'd covered a dog shelter that wasn't treating the animals right. They were crowded, dirty, underfed, and naturally I was outraged."

The mistreatment of animals would have outraged him as well, but Regina was so softhearted, so genuine, he could imagine how emotional she'd gotten over the whole thing.

"The article I did was small, but it ended up getting a lot of attention. The shelter got shut down and heavily fined. With the help of the paper, I spearheaded a campaign to find homes for all the dogs. We eventually succeeded. I would have loved to have kept a few of them myself, but I had no hopes of getting my own home then, and a small apartment is no place for a dog."

Riley looked down at Butch. The dog peeked at him, turned his head to lick Riley's hand and stretched. Riley grinned. "Unless the dog is really small."

Regina smiled, too. "Look at him. He's already fond of you."

Hearing that special soft tone in her voice gave Riley an idea. He could get closer to her by getting closer to her dog. "He knows I respect him. But I imagine if I touched you right now, he'd go right back to bristling." Riley gave her a long, intimate look. "He's going to have to learn to share. But I'll be patient—with him and you."

Regina's lips parted. She caught her breath, then looked at his mouth.

Oh, she was begging to be kissed. Unable to resist, Riley slowly leaned toward her.

He ended up kissing the dog when Butch leaped up between them. He nipped at Riley's mouth and nose, making an awful racket.

"You ungrateful mutt." Mindful of his intentions, Riley kept his tone friendly instead of irritated. Seeing that no kissing would occur, the dog resettled himself against Riley and gave him a big-eyed innocent look.

Regina smothered a laugh. "How could anyone ever hurt an animal? I can't understand it. I don't regret what happened with the shelter, but afterward the owners showed a lot of animosity toward me. Of course, that's understandable because I started the ball rolling that eventually lost them their business. The thing is, unless they just wanted to harass me, they wouldn't make likely suspects because I don't have anything they'd want to steal."

Riley tried to let the pieces come together naturally in his mind, but he knew Regina was right. He was too personally involved. All he could think of was how she might have been hurt worse. "Is there anyone else you can think of who'd dislike you?"

"Why would anyone dislike me?"

That made him grin. "Why indeed? Any problems

with the people you work with? Why did you move here?"

The careful way she masked her expression told him he'd hit a nerve. "I got along with almost everyone at work."

"*Almost* everyone?"

She folded her hands in her lap. "There was one guy who was pretty persistent in trying to get me to go out with him. The more I refused, the more hostile he got."

"You left because of him?"

"Partially. He started showing up at my place at odd hours, watching me all the time. But he wasn't a threat, just a pest. Mostly I left because I thought I might be safer here. I hate to admit to being a coward, but I got spooked. I'm not used to being hit—"

"Hell, I would hope not."

"—and when that man slugged me, that was more than enough for me. I had to wear sunglasses for a week before the bruise faded enough that I could hide it with makeup. So I quit my job, relocated here in Chester and got hired on with the local paper."

Wishing he could get his hands on not only the man who'd dared to strike her, but the weasel who'd hassled her at work, too, Riley shook his head. "And you still found yourself in trouble."

"Right. Unless, as the local police say, it's just a coincidence. Maybe the fire was an accident."

Any time Riley thought of the damn fire, his guts cramped. "I don't think so, Red."

"You don't? Why?" And then she asked with suspicion, "Riley Moore, do you know something I don't know?"

Careful not to disturb the dog, he touched her cheek and gave her a tender smile. "I probably know lots of things you don't know, especially about dangerous situations. But specifically about the fire, no."

"Then why?"

"I dunno. It's just that the day of the fire, you were so jumpy, so nervous. Call it women's intuition, gut instinct, or just caution, you seemed to instinctively know something was about to happen."

"I did feel especially edgy. It felt like people were watching me."

"Maybe they were." After she'd left Riley that day, he couldn't shake off the picture of her nervousness. And her nervousness had become his, until he knew he wouldn't be able to relax for worrying about her. "That sort of thing can be felt," he murmured, more to himself than her.

"That's why you were trailing me?"

"Yeah." He'd known she was meeting Ethan to complete her interview, so he'd gone along, hanging back so that no one would notice him, but close enough to keep an eye out for her. When she'd met up with Rosie first and the two of them had gone to the firework's dealership, his edginess had increased. With good reason.

"I'm glad you followed me," she said. "If you hadn't, who knows what might have happened."

The alarms had brought Ethan to the scene, only he'd thought Rosie was still inside the building. He would have gone in after her if Riley hadn't held him back. Regina and Rosie would have been safe, but Ethan would have died.

Riley shook off the awful memories, then touched the corner of Regina's mouth. It looked tender and ripe and he wanted to kiss her, but first they had to talk. "I was feeling territorial even then." He watched her eyes darken and smiled to himself. "I wish like hell I'd gotten my hands on the bastard who carried you out. He's probably the one who stole your camera."

"Likely, since I'd taken some good photos of the fire hazards. If only I'd realized how serious those hazards were, I could have saved poor Ethan a terrible scare."

"And me as well."

"You?"

"Damn right." The picture of her sitting on the curb, blood on her forehead, her eyes dazed, would stay with him for a lifetime. "I felt like I'd taken a kick to the stomach."

"You didn't look scared. Not like Ethan."

"I'd already found you, and though you were hurt, I knew you were going to be okay. Ethan thought Rosie was in the fire." And he'd been a madman, fighting to go inside after her even though it would have meant his own death. Once Rosie had shown up, having left the building on her own by an upstairs window in the back, Ethan had just collapsed. To this day, Ethan trembled when anyone mentioned the fire. Oh, he was still a fireman, still did his duty with fearless determination, but you didn't mention the fire that almost took Rosie from him.

Riley didn't ever want to be so afraid that he lost all reason and discipline. Which was why he was taking matters into his own hands. He didn't love Regina the way Ethan loved Rosie, but he liked her, he wanted her and for as long as he held a claim, he'd damn well keep her safe.

He dropped his hand. "Maybe I'm just buying into your fears, but its possible you have a good reason to be afraid. I'm not willing to put it to chance."

She pressed back against the couch cushions. "You say that like it has some hidden meaning or something."

"It does." He stared at her hard, keeping her pinned in his gaze. "Regina, I don't want you by yourself until we figure out what's going on."

It took her a second to catch his meaning, then her eyes slanted his way in speculation. "You think you should stay with me?"

"If you move from the apartment, yes."

"No."

He went on as if she hadn't voiced the denial. "Here you're surrounded by people. Help is only a few feet away and anyone could hear you through the thin walls. In a house, you'd be all alone."

Her shoulders straightened. "I'm a big girl, Riley. I'll be extra careful. But I won't—"

"You can't be careful enough. Do you intend to be home before dark every day? And what does it even matter when by your own admission, you've been attacked during the day? You can't imagine how many ways an intruder can get into your house without you even knowing."

Her slim brows pulled down.

"What if someone doesn't want to steal from you at all? What if someone just wants revenge?"

She pushed to her feet to pace away. Riley noticed

her hands had curled into fists at her sides, evidence that she'd had the same worry. "Stop it. You're trying to scare me."

Riley set the dog beside him and stepped up behind her. "Bullshit. I *am* scaring you. And you know why, Red? Because you're smart enough to know I'm right." He clasped her upper arms and pulled her back against his chest. Her hair smelled sweet. *She* smelled sweet. And soft and female and delicate. She demolished his control and intentions without even trying.

Riley pressed his jaw against her temple, and in a roughened voice, said, "Will you check every room, every closet, under every bed and in every corner each night when you first go in? What will you do if you find someone, crouching in the dark, waiting for you?"

Jerking around to face him, she said again, "*Stop it.*"

His hands closed over her shoulders and he brought her to her tiptoes. "The hell I will. You say the threat is real. I believe you. So don't be dumb, Regina."

"What am I supposed to do?" She was so shaken, she practically wailed, then thumped him solidly on the chest. "Hide? Stop living? I have work and friends and errands...."

He caressed her tense shoulders. "Let me help."

"By moving in?" She shook her head. "No, I won't do that. It wouldn't be—"

"Proper? Screw proper. Who's going to know besides our friends?" She started to walk away from him and Riley crushed her close. Her eyes flared. "Improper beats the hell out of dead any day."

The dog started barking, anxiously looking for a way

off the couch. But he was too small to try jumping down.

"You're upsetting my dog."

"Misery loves company." He kissed her, hard at first, but when she went immobile, then soft and sweet against him, he gentled. Her hands curled against his chest, telling him she liked the kiss almost as much as he did. He caught her face, held her still while he sank his tongue in. Her heartbeat pounded against his chest, her soft moan vibrated between them.

Riley carefully pulled back. Her eyes stayed closed, her lips parted. "Listen to me, Red. I'll do everything I can to figure this out before you're due to move. I swear it. But I don't want you living alone."

Her eyelashes fluttered, lifted. Slowly, comprehension dawned and she looked beyond him, then stepped away to scoop up the dog. With her back to Riley, she went about soothing Butch. "If you're that close, you know what will happen."

"We'll sleep together." He crossed his arms over his chest, anxious for it to happen, wondering if she'd admit it.

"Every time you touch me, I forget who I am."

"Meaning?"

"Meaning I'm not the type to get carried away with the moment, but when you're kissing me, it doesn't seem to matter."

She would be ready, more than ready, by the time he got her in bed. He'd see to it. "It's going to happen no matter what, Red. You know that."

She swallowed, then nodded. "I know." She looked

none too pleased with that admission, making Riley frown.

A real gentleman would have told her not to worry about it, that he'd control himself, protect her. He wasn't that much of a gentleman, and he wanted her too much to start playing one now. "We'll go slow." As slow as he could manage, considering he'd held himself at bay for weeks already.

She walked over to the balcony doors and looked out. "I'm sorry. I don't mean to be...coy. It's just that I can't be cavalier about sex."

Her honesty was refreshing, something he hadn't expected. "You don't need to apologize to me for speaking your mind. But we're both adults, both uninvolved." When she didn't look at him, he said, "I don't mean to push you..."

Her laugh sounded strained. "That's all you do is push."

His smile caught him by surprise. "For your safety, yeah. But I'm not cavalier about sex either. No one in their right mind is these days."

"Then I know a lot of men not in their right mind."

He wouldn't think about her with other men. It'd make him nuts. But he could be honest in return. "I can't promise not to touch you, Red, because I will."

Her shoulders lifted on a deep breath. She waited, anxious and still.

Seeing her response, Riley took two steps closer. "Is it worth your safety? Is avoiding me worth risking your life?" And because he knew she already loved her little dog, he pressed her, saying, "Is it worth risking Butch's life?"

He waited, and finally she turned. She looked sad, resigned. "No. I tried ignoring the threat. I tried to believe it was all coincidence like everyone said. I wanted to just go on with my life, keep doing what I always did, keep working." She shook her head and said in a nearly soundless whisper, "I almost got Rosie killed."

Riley knew she still felt guilty for allowing Rosie to be involved, even though everyone knew Rosie did just as she pleased. Ethan couldn't control her, so it was for certain that Regina would never sway Rosie from something she chose to do.

"I know the risks now, but the thing is, Riley, I can't just hide away. I love my job and I won't give it up. Yet, that's when a lot of things seem to happen. Out of control cars, purse snatchers..."

"I have an idea about that, too." A stupid idea, one he was sure to regret, but damn it, he had to be certain she was safe. "You wanted to interview me."

Sudden excitement lit her eyes. Both she and the dog stared at him, she with delighted surprise, Butch with mere curiosity.

After clearing his throat, Riley forged on. "Well, here's your chance. I'm on vacation for the next two weeks. While you finish up any current assignments, I'll accompany you—and no, there's no negotiating on that point, not if you want to interview me next."

"That's blackmail," she pointed out, but she didn't sound too upset about it.

"Take it or leave it."

For three heart-stopping seconds she hesitated. Her slow smile gave him warning. "I'll take it."

Already dreading it, Riley nodded. She sounded enthusiastic enough to make his stomach clench. "During the evening we'll work on your training. I want you to have at the very least a basic understanding of self-defense. While you're still in the apartment, I'll check into the things that've happened to you to see if I can turn up anything."

"But hasn't it been too long?"

"Maybe. But maybe not. Cops file all their reports, so I'll check through that and see if anything jumps out at me. Back when things first happened, they were looking at each incident with the thought that you were a hysterical woman. I'll look with the thought that you're in danger. Two very different perspectives."

She licked her lips. "It happened in Cincinnati, not Chester."

"Don't worry. I'll find what I need to get started."

Still she stood there.

Riley touched her cheek. "Try not to fret, okay? Everything will work out."

"And if you haven't found out anything when it's time for me to move?"

He'd have kissed her again, but Butch started a low rumbling, ears back, body poised to attack. The little dog had enough to get used to without worrying that Riley was accosting his new mistress. "Then you'll continue to stay with me."

"With you? But I thought you—"

"Intended to move in with you? No. My place is already secure. And look at it this way, you can use the time to get your new home up and running." And in the interim, he'd have her—in his home, under his protection and in his bed.

The setup worked for him.

4

BUTCH DIDN'T LIKE sleeping alone.

Regina found that out after a long night of listening to pitiful howls that finally broke her down. At two in the morning she gave up, retrieved Butch from his pen in the warmest corner of her kitchen, and carried him to bed.

He did a reconnaissance of the perimeter, sniffing every corner of her bed, her pillow, the sheets, before crawling under the covers. She watched the lump move here and there, then finally settle close to her. He dug—*endlessly*. She had no idea what he thought he was doing, but he ignored her pleas to stop and finally curled up behind her knees. She couldn't move without making him grumble.

For a four-pound dog, he was sure bossy about his comfort.

At six, when her alarm went off, Butch scampered out, yawned hugely in her face, then wanted to play. When Regina only blinked at him, he reared back on his haunches, barked and nipped her on the nose. She groaned, which he took for a sign of life and started bouncing around the covers like a tiny rabbit. He could stop and start so fast, darting this way and that, it was comical. Even half-asleep, she grinned as he raced up to her, gripped the edge of her pillowcase in his teeth, and began tugging.

"Okay, okay." It was a sorry truth, but she wasn't a morning person. She'd tried over the years to become one, only because it seemed like the thing to do. Good, honest people went to bed at a decent hour and rose early to begin their day. They didn't lie around for hours, being lazy.

Well, she was decent and honest, but she just couldn't force herself to be alert first thing. It took her at least two hours and a pot of coffee to get her head together. Before that, she didn't want to face the world. And with the way she looked in the morning, she doubted the world wanted to face her.

Moving around in the dark, she made a quick trip to the bathroom, turned on the coffeepot, which she'd prepared the night before, and put Butch out on his lead so he could potty. Because the morning was damp that late July day, he finished in a flash.

With only a dim light on over the sink, she slumped at the table in her cozy cotton jammies, nursing her first steaming mug of caffeine. Butch curled in her lap, content just to be with her—until a knock sounded on her door.

She froze.

Butch did not.

In what she now considered typical Butch frenzy, he leaped from her lap and ran hell-bent for the door. He made so much noise, she knew any thoughts of ignoring her early-morning caller were shot. Through the peephole, she spied Riley standing impatiently in her hallway, and she ducked away as if he might see her, too. Good God. What was he doing at her door so early?

"Open up, Red. I can hear Butch, so I know you're up and about."

No. A thousand times no. Still plastered to the side of the door, her heart racing, she croaked, "What do you want?"

"You," he said with a discernable smile in his voice. "But I'll settle for conversation."

Eyes closing in mortification, she shook her head. "Not at six-thirty, Riley. Go away till eight." She could be ready by eight. It'd be rushing it since she usually didn't leave for work till eight-thirty, but under the circumstances—

"Not happening, Red. Now open the door." And then he tacked on, "I have a gift for Butch."

"You do?" She chanced another peek out the peephole and saw that Riley held up a stuffed Chihuahua toy. It looked almost like Butch, but bigger and not as cute. She covered her face with her hands. The man had brought her dog a present. She groaned, undecided.

Beside her, Butch continued to encourage her with barks and jumps and circles. She pressed her forehead to the door. "If I let you in, will you not look at me till I've had a chance to get down the hall?"

Riley laughed. "Why?" And then in a throaty tone, "What are you wearing, Red?"

Regina looked down at herself. Sloppy, blue-flowered cotton pajamas hung on her body. Her loose, tangled hair fell in her face. Even without a mirror, she knew that her eyes were puffy and still heavy from sleep.

"I'm waiting."

This was ridiculous. Half her neighbors would hear him if she didn't do something quick. She flipped on the entry light, turned the locks and cracked the door open. "Riley?" she said in a harsh whisper.

"Yeah?"

"You can come in, but I mean it, don't you dare even think to look at me. I'm a mess and I don't like it when people see me a mess."

"All right, honey, calm down. I promise."

She could hear the laughter in his tone. "The door is unlocked, so just give me thirty seconds to—"

Behind her, the shattering of glass disturbed the early morning quiet.

Screeching, Regina whirled around to see the devastated ruins of her patio doors. Shards of glass glittered everywhere. "Oh my God." She snatched up Butch, who had tucked in his tail and darted behind her before yapping hysterically.

Riley stormed in, moved her to the side and took in the mess in one sweeping glance.

"Close and lock this door, then call the cops." He tossed the stuffed toy dog on the couch, and sprinted across the floor, through the broken patio doors and, to her amazement, right over the balcony.

"*Riley.*" They were only about eight feet up from the ground, but still... Regina slammed her door shut and started after him, but she was barefoot and there was glass scattered everywhere, all over her floor, some atop her furniture. Her heart hammered so hard, it hurt.

Cautiously, she stepped up onto the couch, Butch clutched in her arms. "Ohmigod, ohmigod, damn you, Riley, ohmigod..." She stepped off the other end of the couch nearest to her kitchen. Being careful to avoid any sharp shards of glass, she went to the phone and dialed 9-1-1.

In less than two minutes that seemed like a lifetime, Riley was back. This time he climbed up and over the balcony railing. Regina didn't have a chance to worry about her appearance because he barely spared her a glance. "I need a flashlight. It's still too dark out there to see and I don't want to mess up any evidence."

Skin prickling with sick dread, Regina pointed to the middle of the floor. "It was a rock."

Riley nodded. "I know, honey. Where's a flashlight?"

Flashlight? She felt shocked, disoriented. She hadn't had near enough coffee.

"Regina?"

One deep breath, and she felt marginally more in control. "In my bedroom, in the nightstand drawer."

"Stay put." His booted feet crunched over the remains of her patio door. An early-morning breeze blew the curtains in. The blackness beyond the doors seemed fathomless, sending a chill down her spine.

Belatedly, Regina remembered what else was in her nightstand drawer. *Oh no.* Her heart dropped into her stomach and she started across the floor in a rush, the glass forgotten.

Riley reappeared. Not by look or deed did he acknowledge anything he might have uncovered beyond the flashlight. He crossed to her and handed her a housecoat and slippers.

"You okay?"

Maybe. "Yes."

He cupped the side of her face, his touch gentle and reassuring. "The cops should be here any second. Tell them I'm out back. I don't want to get shot by some overeager hero."

Shot! "Riley, wait." She closed her hand around his arm above his elbow. His muscles were bunched, thick with tension. To someone who didn't know him better, he might almost appear calm. But Regina noted the unfamiliar, killing rage in his blue eyes. He felt warm and strong and secure and she didn't want him to walk away from her.

As if he understood, he bent down to look her in the eyes and said with deadly calm, "It's okay, Red. I know what I'm doing. I want you and Butch to wait in the kitchen."

"No. Don't go out there."

Riley scrutinized her. "You should put on more coffee. The officers will appreciate it."

Coffee? That sort of made sense. At least, with her mind in a muddle, it did. "Oh. Right."

For one brief moment, his gaze moved over her, touching off a tidal wave of warmth. He paused at her mouth, her breasts, then shook his head in chagrin. "Be right back."

Butch squirmed to be let down, but she didn't dare, not with so much glass on the floor. A sort of strange numbness had set in. She blocked the kitchen off with his small pen, pulled on her robe and fuzzy slippers, and went about making more coffee by rote.

This time the knock on her door didn't startle her.

Holding Butch like a security blanket, his small warm body somehow comforting, she skirted the glass and made her way to the door again. Two officers in uniform greeted her. Young, fresh-faced and eager at the prospect of a crime, they looked the complete opposite of Riley. Regina wanted to groan.

Butch wanted to kill them both.

His rabid beast impersonation was especially realistic this time. Regina tried, but there was no shushing him, so she gave up.

At her invitation, the officers cautiously ventured inside, keeping their eyes on Butch. The first officer removed his hat, then nodded at the dog. "What is that?"

Here we go again, Regina thought. "My dog, Butch."

"What's wrong with him?"

"He doesn't like you." Regina closed the door behind them. "Would you like coffee?"

They looked at each other, then her. "Uh, sure." They had to speak loudly to be heard over Butch's furor. "Maybe after you tell us what happened here?"

"Oh." She looked behind her at the devastation. "A rock. Riley Moore is out back poking around with a flashlight. Don't shoot him."

"Riley?" The darker-haired officer lifted one brow. "Why's he here?"

"He was, uh..." Why had Riley dropped in? Oh yeah, a gift for the dog. "Visiting Butch."

"That right?" The two cops shared another look, this time of masculine comprehension.

Regina pulled herself together enough to fry them both with her censure. "Riley is a friend," she stated, emphasizing the last word. "He had just knocked on the door when the rock came crashing in."

At that moment, Riley opened the door behind them and stepped inside. His brows were down, his eyes glittering. "I thought I told you to lock this."

"I did, but then they arrived." She gestured at the officers and shrugged.

Riley glanced at both men. "Dermot, Lanny. Thanks for coming over."

The men looked like little boys next to Riley. Regina allowed herself a moment to appreciate the differences, then said again, "Coffee?"

Riley nodded. "Thanks, babe." He kissed her full on the mouth, annihilating her previous claims of friendship. "We'll be right there."

He wanted to dismiss her? Oh no. She squared her shoulders, but it wasn't easy with Butch putting on such a show.

Almost without thought, Riley took the dog from her. "Good dog." He stroked Butch's back, found just the right spot behind his big ears, and Butch magically quieted. He kept a narrowed gaze on the officers, but the awful racket ended.

Regina turned on her heel and stalked away, muttering under her breath about pigheaded males of both the human and animal variety. From her position in the kitchen, she could hear the men talking in muted tones.

Riley waited, giving the officers a chance to look around. The one he'd called Lanny shone a flashlight over the small balcony—the balcony Riley had jumped from—and shook his head before meandering out there. He came back in and looked around the floor at the broken glass.

"Better call someone to fix that window," Dermot said. "Damn vandals."

"The work of kids, no doubt," Lanny added. "No one supervises them anymore. In my day, my mother would have taken a broom to me for a prank like this."

By the time the officers entered the kitchen, Regina had four mugs out, silverware, a crystal sugar bowl and a matching pot of creamer. "Have a seat, please," she told them.

Lanny nodded. "Thanks." Then, apparently disappointed that he couldn't do more, he said, "I'll take a report, but whoever did this is long gone."

Riley leaned back in his seat, noticeably silent. He continued to stroke Butch who kept looking up at him adoringly, turning his head to get a new spot scratched.

Dermot doctored his coffee, took a long drink, then asked, "You didn't get hurt, did you? The rock didn't hit you?"

Regina shook her head. "No. I'm fine."

Dermot shook his head. "I'm sorry, Ms....?"

"Foxworth. Regina Foxworth."

"Right. You did the right thing calling us but unfortunately, there's not much we can do other than have a squad car drive by and keep an eye on things for the rest of the night."

Same old song, Regina thought. "I understand."

"Well, I don't." Riley blew out a sigh of disgust. "Neither of you went outside to look around the complex."

Dermot frowned at him. "For what? It was a rock."

Lanny nodded. "You know how it is, Riley. We get crap like this all the time."

"No, you don't. And even if you did, that's no excuse for not being thorough."

New tension filled the air. Tones and posture abruptly changed. Lanny was the first to speak up. "Look, Riley, I know you have more training, but—"

"But nothing. I went outside. I looked—just as you should have done. Someone was outside her window for about an hour, just watching."

Regina straightened in new alarm.

"Not a group of unruly kids, but one man. He's a patient son-of-a-bitch, too, and I personally think he was waiting for her to be awake to throw that damn rock."

With sudden clarity, Regina said, "It was right after I turned the light on." She stared at Riley. "Before that, I'd been drinking my coffee in the dark."

"He probably thought it'd shake you up more to catch you when you first woke up." Riley glanced at Regina with an expression close to satisfaction. "Didn't rattle you too much though, did it, honey?"

He sounded teasing, which she didn't understand at all. She calmly sipped her coffee and hoped only she noticed how her hands shook. "No."

Riley smiled, a secret, intimate smile. Turning back to the two men, the smile disappeared to be replaced with a scowl. "If you'd checked, you'd know Ms. Foxworth has a recent history of threatening incidents. In light of that, I don't think anything, especially a rock through her window at dawn, should be taken lightly."

Lanny didn't like the criticism. "Sounds to me like you're personally involved here."

"I am."

Regina nearly choked on her coffee. Why didn't he just take out an ad in the paper? He could tell more people that way.

"But that's irrelevant." Riley wasn't through lecturing. "What pisses me off the most is that neither of you did your job." He encompassed them both in a look.

Regina thought it might be a favorable time to intercede before Riley got too insulting. She pushed back her chair. "Good grief, Riley, have you had breakfast? Surely, a temper like that is wrought from hunger. Would you like some pancakes? Lanny, Dermot? I can put a batch together if you'd like."

Riley stared at her in disbelief. "You're not going to feed them."

"I am if they're hungry." Her chin lifted. "Pancakes would give you something to chew on besides two officers who are only trying to do their duty."

His expression darkened. "They're not doing it very well."

"It's my fault that I didn't mention the other incidents, not theirs."

"Victims get rattled and forget important details. An officer is supposed to know that and ask pertinent questions."

Regina sucked in a breath at the insult. "Are you saying I'm rattled?"

Dermot stood, interrupting the escalating argument. "So how'd you come to all these brilliant conclusions, Riley? That's what I want to know."

Almost in slow motion, his movements rigid and calculated, Riley came to his feet and handed a sleepy Butch to Regina. With his gaze on Dermot, he said, "I'll take pancakes. They'll be leaving—after I explain."

Seeing no hope for it, Regina stepped out of the line of fire.

Riley took a step closer to Dermot, which had the other man's eyes flaring a bit in alarm. "There's damn near a pack of cigarette butts below her window. Red doesn't smoke—"

"Red?"

Regina raised her hand. "He means me."

"Oh." Dermot cleared his throat, glanced at her hair. "Yeah, I guess that makes sense."

In a voice raised to regain attention, Riley continued. "—so they sure as hell aren't hers, but they were fresh, one still smoldering. You know what that means, Dermot?"

Again, he cleared his throat. "Uh, that someone was out there just a few moments ago?"

"There's also one set of prints in the ground. Big adult-size prints. There are no rocks in the apartment landscaping the size of the one now in her living room, so whoever threw it probably brought it with him, meaning this was premeditated, not just a last-minute bit of mischief."

Both officers looked dumbfounded and a little awed.

"Can you maybe get some prints off the rock?"

Riley shook his head. "To get prints, surfaces need to be smooth. Since the rock isn't, there's no point in checking it."

"So what have we got?"

"Speculation. When I stand outside, about twenty feet from the balcony, I can see right into her living room. I think he watched, and saw her light come on."

"I let the dog out before that."

Riley slued his gaze her way. "With a light?"

"Um, no."

Riley nodded in satisfaction. "You need a floodlight out there, Red. And you should never open your door in the dark."

Lanny put his hands on his hips and dropped his head forward. "Okay, so you're a big-shot crime scene tech." He looked up, eyes narrowed. "We're not."

"Learn." That one word fell like a ton of bricks, discomfiting both officers.

Silence throbbed in the kitchen, making Regina more edgy than ever. "I think I'll make those pancakes now."

"Make plenty. I'm starving." Riley didn't spare her a glance as he led both officers to the front door, where he gave them the information they needed to file a report. Regina could just make out the low drone of their voices.

Now wide awake, she mixed up pancake batter with a vengeance. She thought of everything she now had on her to-do list: clean up glass, vacuum her furniture, have the glass replaced in her door... She probably needed to call into work because she'd surely be late.

Butch sat at her heels, staring up at her, just waiting for her to sit down again so he could reclaim her lap. Whenever she glanced at him, his eyes widened hopefully and he wagged his skinny tail in encouragement. Regina shook her head. "There won't be much sitting for me today, sweetie."

Riley strode back in just as she'd pulled out a skillet and set it on the stove top. He didn't stop at the table, though, or even slow down. Startled, Regina drew back as he stalked right up to her, his long legs carrying him quickly to her. He pulled her close and without hesitation, without warning, took her mouth with a surprising hunger that completely caught her off guard.

His big hands, hot and callused, held her upper arms, straining her upward. His head was bent so that his mouth fit hers completely. His lips pressed hard, parting hers, and his tongue thrust in, deep and damp and insistent.

Regina hung in his grip, a little stunned, quickly warmed. Her heartbeat thundered in her ears. He changed position, gathering her to him with one arm tight around her waist so that his other hand could tangle in her hair, tipping her head farther back. He rubbed against her, groaned, then lifted his mouth enough for her to catch her breath.

Against her lips, he murmured, "Christ, you look good."

"Hmm?" With almost no effort, he aroused her to the point of incomprehension.

Damp, warm, openmouthed kisses were pressed to her throat, along her shoulder where the robe had opened and the loose neckline where her pajamas drooped....

Her pajamas.

"Riley!"

He held her head in his hands, brushed her cheeks with his thumbs. In a rushed voice, hoarse and low, he said, "You're beautiful."

Beautiful? Regina blinked over such an absurd comment. Her hair was a mess, more so now that he'd tunneled his fingers through it. Her eyes were sleep-heavy and she had not a single speck of makeup on. The pajamas were comfortably baggy, not in the least attractive. "I...I need to go get dressed."

Slowly, he shook his head. "No. I like you just how you are." He kissed her again before she could argue. This kiss was deeper, hotter. She was aware of so many things—the press of his strong fingers on her skull, keeping her immobile, the heat of his breath, the taste of him.

His tongue retreated, moved over her lips, then licked into her mouth again. When his hands released her head, she kept the kiss complete, unable to get enough of him. His tongue retreated, hers followed. His sank in again and she sucked at it.

She knew his hands were roving over her, not stroking her breasts as he had done before, so she didn't understand what he was doing—until her robe fell open and he pushed it aside.

Oh, but it was hard to think with Riley holding her so close, touching her in such remarkable ways. He smelled delicious this morning, like soap and the outdoors and like himself. He was so warm, the cotton of his T-shirt so soft over solid muscle. His callused fingertips slipped beneath the hem of her pajama top to trace the indentation of her waist, then higher, until he teased just beneath her breasts. He circled, glided over and under her nipples, not touching them but bringing her breasts to a tingly, almost acute sensitivity. She held her breath, wanting more, wanting everything.

In the next instant, his thumbs brushed up and over her nipples. The touch was so electric, so anticipated, she jolted against him, gasped, and her fingers bit into his upper arms, closing on rock-solid muscles.

Regina didn't want him ever to stop touching her; if anything, she wanted more and tried to tell him so by pressing closer with a soft moan. Though he hadn't touched her below the waist, her whole body sang with awareness. Her thighs trembled, her belly had filled with butterflies and a curling, undulating sensation of ripe pleasure expanded and retreated within her.

Riley removed his hands, then drew her head to his shoulder, rocking her a little, rubbing her back in a soothing, calming way.

She didn't understand. "Riley?"

"I have to stop, Red. When you agree to sleep with me, I want you to be totally clearheaded, so you won't have regrets."

Regina didn't know what he was muttering about. She pressed her nose into his throat and breathed in his warm male scent, filling herself up. She wanted to taste his skin, but knew that might not be wise.

Against her ear, Riley rumbled, "While you fix the pancakes, I'll clean up the glass and call someone to replace the door." His tongue touched her ear, traced the rim, dipped inside. Little shivers of excitement raced along her arms and nape and she almost melted. "After breakfast you can pack."

The fog thinned. "Pack?"

"Yeah." His hard hand drifted lower, all the way to the base of her spine. He pressed gently—and she felt his erection against her belly, long, hard.

Regina shoved back. "What do you mean, *pack?*"

As if she should have already understood, Riley held her face turned up to his so she couldn't miss his frown. His gaze bore into hers, insistent, unrelenting. "You can't stay here now."

When she still stared at him in confusion, his frown became a black scowl. "Red, someone is getting pretty bold. And if that doesn't alarm you, then look at Butch."

She glanced down at the dog. He had his tiny front paws crossed over Riley's big foot with his head resting on them. His big brown eyes stared up at her trustingly. He was so shaken, he hadn't even protested their intimacy.

"Do you really want to chance letting him outside to do his business again, knowing someone could be lurking there, that they might snatch him away or, worse, use him to upset you?"

She knew what he was saying, and her heart squeezed tight. "*No.*" In a protective rush, Regina scooped him up and hugged him to her breasts. He twisted and rubbed against her, luxuriating in the human attention. She needed the comforting contact as much as her dog did.

"Look at him," Riley said, "he's still shaking."

Without removing her cheek from the dog's neck, she said, "He always shakes and you know it." She had a feeling Riley only used the dog as leverage, and still she had to admit he was right. She'd be heartsick if anything happened to him. He trusted her to keep him safe, to take care of him, and she intended to do just that.

"I have plenty of room." Riley watched her with a sort of cautious regard. "You'll be safer with me."

Regina looked past him, through the kitchen doorway. The sun was on the rise, a crimson ball that reflected like fire on every sharp, jagged shard of glass littering her once secure home. She chewed her lip in indecision, but no other option came to her. If she went with him, it wouldn't be just an agreement to share space, and she knew it. It'd be an agreement to start an affair.

Her heart pounding for an entirely different reason now, she glanced at Riley, drew a breath, and said, "All right."

Riley encompassed both her and Butch in a bear hug. Butch bit his nose.

Now that he'd gotten his way, Riley grinned like a rascal. "You really do look great in your pajamas and with your hair all loose and tangled." He fingered one long curl. "Sexy as hell."

Heat rushed up her neck to warm her face. She turned her back on Riley and set the dog down. "I didn't even realize..."

"You were rattled, just as I said."

Regina wanted to groan. She was *still* rattled. "I can't believe I sat there in front of those men..."

"They thought you looked hot, too. I wonder if they think we've been sleeping together."

She slanted him a sharp look. "You tried hard enough to give them that impression."

"No choice. With them both eyeing you, I had to stake a claim." Totally unrepentant, he kissed her ear again and squeezed her waist. "I didn't want them getting any ideas about pursuing you."

Feeling like a fool, Regina smoothed her hair and retied the belt of her robe. "I guess I ought to call work since it looks like I'll be late." She picked up the receiver.

"Go ahead." Riley's blue eyes twinkled with teasing. "While you do that, I think I'll just go put the flashlight back in your nightstand—"

Regina whipped around so fast she almost fell. She grabbed Riley by the back of the shirt. "No."

He cocked a brow. "No?"

She dropped her hands, dusting them nervously across her thighs. "That is, I'll do it." She snatched the flashlight away from him. "You should call about the door."

"Right." And then with feigned confusion, he said, "But I thought you were going to call work."

The unholy grin gave him away, and her temper ignited. "You snooped in my drawer, didn't you?"

"Snooped? Now why would I do that, Red? What are you hiding in there?"

Regina swatted at him, embarrassed, irritated. "You had no right." In a snit, she went past him, stepping over the dog's pen and marching toward her bedroom. Glass crunched beneath her slippers, but she barely noticed.

Riley was right on her heels. "The *Kama Sutra*, Red? That's a little dated, isn't it?" His teasing voice grated along her nerves. "But that other book...what was it called? Oh yeah. *Getting the Most Pleasure in Bed*. Now that's current, right?"

Stopping beside her bed, Regina pointed an imperious finger at the door. "Get out."

He didn't budge. "And no less than a dozen rubbers. Woman, what have you been planning?" He stepped closer, forcing her to back up until her legs hit the side of the mattress. "More importantly, any chance you were planning it with me?"

With sudden clarity, Regina knew he hadn't seen the photo. No, being typically male, he'd only noted the silly books and condoms. "No."

"No, what? You weren't planning anything with me?"

She shook her head, felt silly for going mute, and managed to say again, "No."

His smile turned smug. "I didn't really think so. After all, those condoms are smalls." And totally deadpan, "They'd never fit."

Regina's heart jumped into her throat. She licked suddenly dry lips. "No?"

He shook his head. "I'm just an average man, Regina."

"There's nothing average about you."

His slow smile nearly melted her heart. "Maybe you

should wait until we've made love to make that judgment."

A tidal wave of awareness nearly took out her knees. They were in her bedroom, right next to her unmade bed. Her heart gave a hard thump, then tripped into double time.

Riley stepped closer, a grin playing about his mouth. "Such a pretty blush, Red." He looked at her bed, gave a small shake of his head, and all teasing evaporated. "So tell me, Red. What have you been planning, and with whom?"

No never. Not in a million years. "The books are just...curiosity."

"Curiosity about sex?"

It wasn't easy, but she gave a cavalier shrug. "About...variety." She knew about sex. She even knew about pleasure. But things didn't always go right, no matter how she tried. With an airy wave of her hand, she explained, "I bought the books and condoms months ago, when I was engaged."

"*Engaged?*"

His thunderous expression surprised her. "Yes."

"You were in love with someone?"

He said that like an accusation, confusing her even more. Because he looked so red in the face, she decided to admit the truth. "No, I didn't love him. I thought I *could* love him, and I loved the idea of being married and starting a family...."

He'd grown so rigid, she rushed on to explain. "The engagement ended almost as soon as it began. I realized what a stupid move it was, and he made it plain he didn't love me and likely never would. I think he just used the engagement as a sham, a way to..."

"Get you into bed?"

It sounded so stupid, and she'd been so gullible, that she only shrugged. "The, um, condoms have never been opened. I just haven't had the nerve to throw them out. I didn't want anyone to see them in my garbage."

Slowly, Riley relaxed. His frown smoothed out, replaced by a tender expression that seemed so incongruous to the hard man he could be. "Wouldn't be proper, huh?"

"It's private, that's all."

He started to say more, but Butch gave an impatient howl from the kitchen.

Riley glanced that way, then back at her. "I'll get him." He touched her chin, lifted her face and pressed his mouth to hers for several heart-stopping moments. "You better get dressed before I forget my dubious code of honor and the fact that we have a lot to get done in the next couple of hours." He turned and went through the door.

The second he disappeared, Regina jerked the drawer open, took out the framed photograph and looked around for a good place to hide it. She'd just lifted her mattress, ready to shove it beneath, when Riley stepped back in with a wriggling Butch in his arms. He drew up short when he saw her, then his brows came down.

His gaze went from her guilty face to her hand, which she quickly stuck behind her back. "All right, Red. What are you up to now?"

5

RILEY WATCHED as Regina jerked the framed photo behind her back. Green eyes wide and innocent, she said, "It's nothing."

"Right." He strode forward, watched her quickly back up and move around the bed to the other side, and his suspicions grew. He set the dog on the mattress. Butch ran to Regina, came up on his hind legs and begged to be held.

Without taking her gaze off Riley, she caught the dog up one-handed. "If you'll leave, I'll get dressed."

Riley crossed his arms over his chest, not about to oblige her. "I'm damn curious, Red, what's worth hiding from me when I already saw the dirty books and rubbers."

Her jaw firmed. "They're not *dirty* books, they're educational."

"Uh-huh."

"And it's none of your business."

"Someone is trying to hurt you. Everything is my business."

Her cheeks colored. "This is...personal. Nothing that anyone else would care about."

"You don't trust me."

"Of course I do."

"Then let me see."

"Riley."

She wailed his name, making him smile. Stalking her, he started around the bed. She took one step back, then planted her feet and glared. Butch licked her chin in commiseration. Absently, she patted his back.

She was such an affectionate woman, so soft and gentle. It didn't take much to make her blush—a smile from him, a touch and her cheeks turned pink. The more he was with her the more he wanted her, and the more he wanted to know all her secrets. She'd kept parts of herself away from him, her engagement, her insecurities...but no more.

He stopped right in front of her and held out his hand.

She shook her head in exasperation. "This is stupid."

Riley waited.

Finally, with no graciousness, she slapped the picture frame into his hand. His curiosity keen, Riley turned it over, and was met with the charismatic smile on Senator Welling's face. Riley decided it must be the photo she took in the park, given the fountain beside him and the large trees behind him. Regina had written at the bottom of the photo, *Senator Xavier Welling,* along with the date of the photo.

The senator was easily in his mid-fifties. He was tall, gray-haired and aristocratic. In order to always make a good public appearance, he'd kept in shape. He had no paunch and his shoulders were still wide from his college football days.

Riley saw red. Through stiff lips, he said, "You keep a picture of the senator beside your bed?" And then with jealousy pricking his temper, he added, "Next to the goddamned *Kama Sutra?*"

Regina drew herself up. "Don't raise your voice to me."

It wasn't easy, but Riley reigned in his temper. He tossed the picture onto the bed. "What the hell does it mean?"

"What does what mean?"

"Don't look so confused, Red. You've got his picture in your nightstand drawer, next to your bed, with books on sex and a load of rubbers." Hell, just saying it made him madder. "You got the hots for him?"

She gasped so hard, Butch started to howl again. She absently stroked him. "Of course not. He's a wonderful, respectable man with a wife he loves and a family he cherishes."

"Don't make me puke. He's a politician, first and foremost."

Regina went on tiptoes to poke him in the chest. "Yes, he's a politician. A wonderful senator. He's fought hard for the health and safety of children. He supports local law enforcement. He's won numerous awards and honors for leadership and—"

Riley turned his back on her. "Jesus, you're besotted."

Using her free hand, she caught the back of his shirt. "I am not," she all but shouted. "Senator Welling is an inspiration. I admire him, just as I admire his family and his aspirations and his beliefs." And then, in a smaller voice filled with vulnerability, she said, "I admire everything he stands for."

Riley turned to stare at her, something in her tone

touching deep inside him. "Just what does he stand for, Regina?"

Still disgruntled, Regina chewed her lip, not looking at him. "Family. Community. Everything that's good. When you see him campaigning with his wife and kids, you just know that's how it *should* be, all of them smiling, happy, secure." She lifted her gaze to meet Riley's. "I see them together and I know it can happen, because it's right there, live, real."

Riley didn't know how real a politician's public persona might be, but he could tell Regina believed in it. When she'd talked of her family, she'd done so with very little emotion. He'd found that strange, but hadn't pondered it long, not when most of his thoughts centered on carnal activities.

Feeling like a complete bastard, Riley pulled her into his arms. Butch wiggled until he was up between their faces, making sure no kissing would occur. But Riley felt content just to hold her. At least for now.

"I'm sorry."

Against his chest, she murmured, "For what?"

"For prying. And for not understanding." Keeping one hand on Butch so he wouldn't fall, Riley stroked Regina's back. He wished he could touch her bare silky skin again, but he didn't dare. It had been a close thing in the kitchen, his control severely tested. Only the fact that he knew damn good and well she wasn't thinking straight had kept him from laying her across the kitchen table. She'd been ready, damn it, whether she wanted to admit it or not.

"I guess it's okay," she said while rubbing her cheek

against him, setting him on fire again. "It's not a secret that I admire the senator and what he stands for."

"Looks can be deceiving, you know."

She shook her head. "Being a politician does not automatically make him a fraud, Riley."

"No. But the world is filled with cheats and liars, people you'd bet on in a pinch, who turn out to be more unscrupulous than you ever could have imagined."

Leaning back, she looked at him thoughtfully. "Have you known people like that?"

He skirted that question by stating the obvious. "I'm a cop, Red. I see the worst of mankind all the time."

Her hand smoothed over his chest. She couldn't know how the innocent touch inflamed him. If she did, she wouldn't now be looking at him with so much understanding. "You deal with that element of life. But Senator Welling is just the opposite. He's part of the good team, Riley."

Riley wanted to shake her for her naiveté. He knew firsthand how difficult it was to read the people you cared about. Blind trust was never a good thing, but since he wanted it from Regina, he didn't say so.

Riley tucked a long curl behind her ear. "Can I ask you something, honey?"

She laughed.

"What?" He held her away so he could better see her face.

"You're so funny, Riley. Demanding one minute, requesting the next."

"I'm glad you're amused." He smiled, too. "So is it all right?"

"Sure. At this rate, I won't have any secrets left at all."

That'd suit him just fine. He intended to make her his, but never again would he be made the fool. Knowing everything about her would be a safeguard against unhappy surprises.

He released her and she sat on the bed. Butch circled her lap, then nudged his way beneath her housecoat so he could curl up against her stomach. She tucked him in before looking at Riley in inquiry.

Riley settled himself beside her. "Who footed the bill when your parents died?" If she'd been the only one responsible, it'd help explain her need for doing things right, to always be prepared and proper.

She appeared confused by the question. "I did what I could, but I didn't have enough money to make a huge difference in their care. What I had to give wasn't enough, so instead I spent days researching ways to get them the help they needed. It's wasn't easy. That's one of the things about Senator Welling. His health benefit programs would have done my parents a world of good."

Riley did not want to talk about the damned senator. "What about your brother? Did he help out?"

"I told you, he's just like them. I had to loan him money to buy a suit so he'd have something decent to wear to the funerals."

Damn, that meant she alone had had the burden of her parents' care. "Loan—or give?"

She shrugged, which was all the answer Riley needed. "What about your fiancé? What happened there?"

Hedging that question, she asked, "Just who is the reporter here, Riley? Me or you?"

With a straight face, Riley said, "I just wondered if he could possibly be the one bothering you now." He spoke the truth, but it wasn't the only reason he asked. Possessiveness had a lot to do with his interest, too.

"Oh. No, he didn't help with my parents. Our engagement was after their deaths. And, no, it's not him."

"How do you know for sure?"

She untangled a grouchy Butch from her lap and pushed to her feet. "Trust me. He has no reason to hold a grudge."

Riley took the dog from her. He immediately rooted underneath Riley's shirt, circled into a small ball, and sighed himself back to sleep. Riley looked down at the lump where his flat abdomen used to be, shook his head, and put one hand over the dog. "Men see things differently than women. Maybe your take on the breakup isn't the same as his."

Regina rubbed her head. "It's not. But that has nothing to do with anything."

Her reluctance to talk about the other man couldn't have been more plain. It nettled Riley. "So who did the breaking up, you or him?"

"I did, but he didn't mind."

"How could he not mind? That doesn't make any sense. If he'd asked you to marry him—"

"He didn't want me, all right?" She threw up her hands. "There. Happy? He called me a prude and said I was unappealing. He wanted me to change myself and I can't do that, and he said that no man would want me, especially in bed, and so I *left*. End of story."

Stunned speechless, Riley watched her storm out of the room.

For long minutes after, he remained on the bed, soothing Butch who had gone a little frantic at Regina's raised voice. He'd crawled up Riley's chest, grumbling and growling, then poked his head out the neck of the shirt, just beneath Riley's chin. "Her fiancé sounds like a complete ass, doesn't he, Butch?"

Butch whined.

"I wonder, is that why she bought the books? Had she already realized that things weren't going well between them? Not that I'm sorry to hear it, because if she hadn't, she might have married him."

Butch whined a little louder.

"I agree." Riley had to take off his shirt to get Butch free. "Does she still love the guy, do you think?"

Butch had no answer.

When Riley entered the kitchen, Regina was on the phone with her editor, explaining about the glass. She didn't look at Riley, and after she hung up, she went past him to the living room.

"I won't be going in today at all. Most of the work I need to do for the rest of my assignment can be handled on the phone and typed up on my computer." She paused. "Is it okay if I bring my computer?"

Riley followed behind her, cautious of her new mood. "You can bring anything you want."

"Thank you." She pulled out a phone book from the closet and carried it back to the kitchen.

"What are you doing?"

"Looking up numbers for glass replacement. I want this fixed before the evening."

Riley followed her. "I'll take care of that."

"You said that half an hour ago."

"This time I mean it." He wrested the book out of her hands and plunked Butch into her arms. The poor dog had been passed around a lot that morning. "Go shower and pack whatever clothes you need right away. I'll call for the door replacement, take you to my place, then come back here and get your computer and any other stuff you need. All right?"

"I am not helpless."

"Far from it." He tried a smile that she didn't return. "C'mon, Red. You look stressed and tired and I want to take care of you just a little, okay?"

She stared up at him for long moments. "I'll finish up my work on this current piece today."

The swift change of topic threw him. "Great."

"That means tomorrow, or even later tonight, I can start my interview on you."

His smile slipped a little, but he managed to hang on to it. "Okay."

"I have so many questions, it might take a few...days."

His smile felt like a grimace. "I did agree."

"Yes, you did." She handed Butch back to him. "Can you keep an eye on him while I shower and dress? Thank you."

Both Riley and Butch watched her leave yet again, her walk a little more sassy this time. Oh, she wanted payback with the interrogation, he could tell. Riley wondered how many answers he could give without telling things he never wanted to reveal? It'd be tricky, but he could handle it.

If all else failed, he'd distract her with a kiss—and more. After all, he'd given her fair warning of what to expect. And still she'd agreed.

That thought brought back his smile in full force. In the end, he'd get what he wanted most: Regina. That made the rest worthwhile.

"WELL, THIS ANSWERS one question, doesn't it?" Regina stated.

Riley had parked his truck behind her Escort in his allotted garage space, then joined her. She stood between the car and the opened door, staring at his apartment.

Unlike most women Riley knew, Regina hadn't lingered in the shower. Butch, unwilling to wait in the kitchen while Riley cleaned up the glass, had howled endlessly until Regina stuck her head out the bathroom door and asked Riley to hand him to her. Butch had curled up on a towel and slept while she quickly showered and dressed in white slacks and a sleeveless cotton sweater and sandals. With her long red hair restrained in a French braid, minimal makeup and small earrings, she looked classy and sexy combined.

A large satchel with files and notes from her current project was slung over her arm. Riley hadn't realized that she gathered so much info just for one story. And since she'd told him her current article was about the silly talent show held by a local television station in the mall, he was doubly surprised.

They'd both driven so Regina would have her car

handy. Not that he wanted her out driving around alone until he figured out what was going on. But neither did he want her to feel trapped or overly dependent on him. He knew she would rebel over that and he'd lose her before he could get her used to being with him.

Butch was on a thin leash, so Riley lifted him out of the car, then took Regina's elbow to move her forward. He closed her car door. "You disappointed?"

"That you don't have your own house?" She glanced at him over her shoulder and smiled. "No, of course not." Then she asked, "But why don't you?"

Riley shook his head. Before meeting Regina, he'd thought he had enough of hearth and home to last him a lifetime. He said only, "This is easier. Less maintenance." He led her and Butch up the walkway. "I'll show you around, then unload your stuff."

All she'd brought this trip were a few changes of clothes, her bedding—because she claimed she needed her own pillow to sleep—Butch's belongings and the material for her current assignment. She'd packed up more stuff at the house and disconnected her computer, but Riley told her he'd get all of that when he returned to meet the glass repairmen. Everything else they could retrieve as needed.

Since his place was on the ground floor, it'd be more convenient for Butch. He only hoped Butch liked the big golden retriever next door, since they'd be sharing yard space. He unlocked the door and pushed it open for Regina to enter.

"Oh, Riley, this is very nice."

He watched her look around. Luckily, he was a tidy

man, otherwise he couldn't imagine her reaction. She touched her hand to the arm of a brown leather sofa, glided her fingers over a marble tabletop. "Did you decorate yourself?"

"Yeah." At the time, he'd taken enjoyment in only pleasing himself, with no one else to consider. He hadn't expected ever again to want the approval of a woman. And Regina wasn't just any woman, but an immaculate one at that.

Only it looked as though Regina liked his choices. "There's only one bath, but we'll work that out." Maybe they could share the shower? He grinned, then covered that reaction by discussing the dog. "I'll hook a lead up for Butch so he can run a little more outside. Oh, and if you need me to pick up any groceries for you, just let me know. I tend to do a lot of fast food."

He tugged Butch inside and closed the door.

Butch's ears perked up with his first glimpse of the place, giving Riley warning. He leaned down to unleash the little rat. In a stern voice, his finger shaking in the dog's face, Riley said, "Now listen up, bud. No piddling on the furniture, okay?"

Rather than feeling intimidated, Butch snapped at his finger, making Riley grin. "I almost forgot, with all the excitement." He pulled the stuffed Chihuahua from his pocket and tossed it toward the middle of the room. Butch jerked about to watch the stuffed animal land, then he reared back on his haunches, did a bunny hop to where the floppy toy lay—and attacked.

Regina started laughing at his antics.

Riley had to admit it was pretty cute the way he shook the toy, threw it this way and that. For such a small dog, he made feral sounds. Then as if expecting it to follow, Butch went into flight. It was so funny to watch him run. Somehow he managed to streamline himself, laying his ears back, tucking in his tail and dashing around furniture and corners so fast he was practically a blur.

His tiny feet made a distinct patter on the wooden floor. He slid around the corner, took a second to get some traction, and was off again.

Regina watched in wonder. "He doesn't know your place yet. How can he be sure he won't run into anything?"

Riley slung his arm around her shoulders, already enjoying having her in his home. "Men have great reflexes."

She cocked a brow at him. "And women don't?"

"Some women do." He pinched her chin, tipped up her face and kissed her mouth. "We'll be working on yours, remember?"

A knock sounded on his door. Regina pulled back in surprise, but Riley just shook his head. He opened the door and there stood Ethan, Rosie, Harris and Buck.

As usual, Rosie was pinned up against Ethan's side, and she appeared most comfortable there.

Harris, a firefighter at the same station as Ethan, looked fatigued, a good indicator that he'd recently come off his shift. Though Riley knew he'd have showered, the scent of smoke still clung to him. He pushed his black hair back with a hand and lounged against the door frame, his blue eyes tired and a little red.

Riley gave him the critical once-over. "Hell, Harris, you look like you should be in bed."

Harris yawned hugely. "Just left bed, actually." His satisfied grin said he'd just left a woman, also.

Riley grunted. "Maybe you should have tried sleeping."

"Did that—*after*. But last night was a bitch so I'm still sluggish."

Ethan nodded. "Had a pileup on the expressway. Three cars caught fire. No one died, thank God, but we worked our asses off."

Buck threw a thick, muscular arm around Harris, nearly knocking him off balance. Being the owner of a lumberyard and used to daily physical labor kept Buck in prime shape and made him the bulkier one in the group. Like Harris, Buck was single and enjoyed playing the field.

Still holding Harris, Buck pulled off a ball cap and scratched his head, further messing his brown hair. Green eyes alight with laughter, he said, "Harris never minds toiling through the night, 'cuz the ladies like to fawn all over him the next day."

"Jealous?" Harris asked.

"Naw." Then with a huge grin and a feigned yawn, he said, "I just got out of bed myself."

Riley laughed and held the door wide open. They all piled in, and Rosie was about to say "hi" when Butch flew around the corner, skidded to a halt, and went into a rampage of spitting Chihuahua fury.

Ethan tucked Rosie close. "What the hell?"

Rosie said, "Oh, it's so cute!"

Harris shrank behind Buck, pretending to cower. "Cute? What is it?"

"Whatever it is," Buck added, "it's demonic."

Riley caught Regina's scowl and laughed. "You might as well get used to hearing that, Red. It seems to be the typical response to your dog."

Buck and Harris said in unison, "Dog? You're kidding, right?"

Riley lifted Butch, who seemed to take extreme dislike to Ethan holding his wife. Most of his ire was directed at him.

"What did I do?" he asked

Rosie laughed, saying, "What haven't you done?"

"Hey." Riley held the dog eye level. "They're friends. You can relax now."

But Butch wasn't having it. Rosie dared to try to pet him and Butch practically went over Riley's shoulder in his effort to escape her. As long as he thought he had everyone cornered, he was as brave as a German shepherd, but let someone reach for him and he tucked his tail quick enough.

Regina took her dog. "He's still getting used to me and Riley. He's...shy."

Buck forced Harris to turn him loose. "Yeah? Is that what you call it?"

"I'd call it rabid," Ethan said.

Now that he was close to Regina, Butch quieted and started to lick her chin. Harris curled his lip. "That's disgusting."

"I think he's adorable."

Harris nudged Buck. "Yeah, Rosie, but you think Ethan is adorable, too, so you obviously have lousy taste."

Riley attempted to get things back on track. "Now that you're here I can explain."

Regina froze. "Explain what?"

"What's going on, of course." He knew she wouldn't like it, but he thought the extra backup wouldn't hurt. "They're friends, Red. And I want Harris and Buck to help me move some of your stuff."

Ethan sent his wife a look, then stared at Riley. "She's moving in with you?"

"Temporarily," Regina rushed to clarify.

At the same time, Riley said, "She is."

Rosie just grinned. "This is great. But what about your house?"

"As soon as it's mine, I'll—"

"As soon as it's *safe*, she'll move in there." Riley didn't want to think about her being on her own like that until he knew for certain that no one would hurt her. "Rosie, why don't you help Red make up the guest bed?" Riley suggested, and saw Harris and Buck start elbowing each other again, "and I'll get these goons to lend a hand unloading."

Rosie frowned. "Why can't Harris help her make the bed? I'd rather hear the scoop."

Harris stepped forward eagerly, eyebrows bobbing. "Oh yeah, I'll help her—"

Riley hauled him back with a hand in his collar. "I need to talk to you." Then to Rosie, "Regina can tell you what's going on."

"Yeah, well, somehow I think I'd hear a different version from you. Guys always have a different version."

Regina looked pained. "Really, I can make the bed myself and there's not that much to carry in."

Ethan grabbed his wife and kissed her. It wasn't a

quick kiss or a timid one. Against her mouth, he teased, "Riley's suffering here, sweetheart. Be agreeable for once, will you?"

Dreamy eyed, Rosie said, "I'm agreeable every night."

Ethan touched her cheek and grinned. "Yes, you are."

Harris rolled his eyes. "God, will the honeymoon never end?"

In a quick mood switch, Rosie reached around her husband and shoved Harris, who fell into Buck. In a huff, she turned and grabbed Regina's arm. "Come on. Let them do the grunt work. You'll probably tell it right where Riley will only beat his chest and play Neanderthal."

That observation had Regina laughing. Butch gave the men a bark of farewell as the women disappeared around the corner.

"Okay," Ethan said, now that they were alone. "What's going on?"

"Outside. I don't want Regina to hear me."

Harris said, "Why is it the second a guy starts really caring about a woman, he complicates things?"

Buck nodded. "It becomes one big soap opera, doesn't it?"

Ethan and Riley hauled them out the door. At Regina's car, Riley said, "Someone is trying to hurt her, or scare her. I'm not sure which, and I don't know why."

Harris leaned on her fender. "No shit?"

"She okay?" Buck asked.

"Yeah. She's hanging in there. Regina is tougher than she looks."

Harris snorted, and when Riley glared at him, he held up his hands in surrender. "Hey, I wasn't casting aspersions on the lady. It's just hard to imagine anything tough about her."

Buck grinned, adding fuel to the fire. "She is a rather soft-looking woman, huh?"

Ethan rolled his eyes. "Quit baiting him, you two. He's got enough on his mind as it is."

All humor vanished when Riley said, "Someone threw a rock through her patio doors this morning." Seeing that he now had their undivided attention, he added, "And that's not all." As quickly as possible, Riley explained what had been happening.

"Could be coincidence," Ethan pointed out. "But I gather by your expression, you don't think so."

"No."

"Any ideas?" Harris asked.

"I'm going to check into her old fiancé. Things ended only a few months ago."

"Regina was engaged?" Ethan looked startled by that disclosure.

"Yeah, and there's some idiot who made a pest of himself at her old job. I'll get names from her tonight." Riley also intended to talk to Senator Welling. That might be a little more difficult to accomplish, but if Welling had seen anything the day her car was run off the road, or if he'd noticed anything suspicious at the park, Riley wanted to know about it. The senator had an appearance scheduled at a ceremony for the historical society. Should be easy enough to grab a few words with him then.

"And in the meantime?" Ethan asked.

"I don't want her alone." Which was the main reason he'd gathered his friends together. He couldn't be with her 24/7, so he'd count on them to help out. "For right now, I figured Rosie could stay here with her while we go get some of her things. Plus, I don't want repairmen in her apartment without supervision. They're due in about an hour."

"If it's not safe, then I don't want Rosie involved."

Riley sent his best friend a long look. "Would I put Rosie in any danger?"

"I wouldn't think so."

"Then relax. They're safe enough here, especially since no one knows Red is staying with me."

Ethan scrutinized Riley. "She says it's temporary."

Riley drew a breath. "For now." And then as he walked back to the apartment carrying Butch's pen and bed, he added, "But I'm working on it."

6

THE SECOND Riley opened her apartment door, he felt the tension. With a raised hand, he shushed the men behind him and stepped silently inside. There was no noise, but the silence was thick, somehow alive. Automatically, Riley's gaze searched out every nook and corner, fast but thorough. He noted the unfamiliar shadow in the bedroom doorway. As he stared, it shifted the tiniest bit and all his senses went on alert.

He flattened his hand on Ethan's chest. In a nearly soundless voice, he ordered, "Stay here."

Ethan took exception to that with a muttered, "Like hell."

Unwilling to waste any time, Riley started into the living area. A floorboard squeaked beneath his foot, and in the next instant motion exploded around him. A crash sounded and a tall, dark man dressed all in black bolted out of the bedroom. In one fluid motion, he went through the patio doors and over the railing, much as Riley had earlier.

Without a second thought, Riley went after him.

Behind him, he heard Ethan yell, "Call the police," and then he was at the railing, cursing as Riley hit the ground. He landed in a crouch on the balls of his feet, took only a single moment to get his balance, and gave pursuit.

The man was several feet in front of him, b t Riley was fast and more than a little determined. Thi; could be the man who'd been terrorizing Regina but, either way, he'd been in her apartment where he didn't be-l ng. Riley could easily take him apart with his bare hands—but he was a cop, and so he'd go by the law. Even if the restraint killed him.

When he'd almost reached the intruder, Riley didn't grab him with his hands. Instead, he kicked cut, sweeping the man's legs out from under him.

The big man went down with a loud grunt of pain. Riley hit hard, too, jarring his bones but unmindful of any pain. He rolled and was atop the other man before the goon could regain his feet. Riley immobilized him by catching his legs with his own, then twisting the man's thick right arm up and back at a very unnatural angle. The man howled in pain. It wouldn't take much pressure to snap a bone or pull the arm from the shoulder socket, and with the way Riley felt, he was more than willing.

Another loud groan issued from his captive.

"Be still," Riley commanded, then he glanced up to see Buck and Harris standing at his side.

Buck curled his lip. "I'm not a cop, Riley. Want me to break something on him?"

The offer was so ludicrous coming from Buck—a man known for laughter, but never aggression—that Riley almost grinned. "If he moves, kick him in the teeth."

"Right." Buck planted his muscular legs apart in what appeared to be anticipation. His size twelve-and-a-half feet were encased in sturdy steel-toed boots.

Wearing a grimace, the intruder twisted to see Riley. "You're a cop?" he gritted out.

"That's right. But I'm off duty. Some uniforms will be here shortly to haul your ass downtown."

"Christ, man, you're breaking my arm."

Harris nodded. "He's right, Riley." He turned his head, contemplating the strange hold Riley had on him. "Looks like you might be breaking a leg, too."

"Don't tempt me." He nudged the guy. "What's your name?" When the man hesitated, Riley growled, "Say it, damn it. Don't make up a lie."

"Earl! My name's Earl."

"Earl what?"

Rather than answer, he groaned in agony.

"Just Earl, huh?" Approaching sirens split the air. Riley said, "Well, Earl, you want to tell me what you were doing in the apartment?"

Sweat beaded on the man's forehead. "Saw it was open. Just wanted to have a look around."

"Right. Let's try again. What were you looking for?"

"Nothing." His head dropped forward to the ground and he panted. "It's the truth, damn it."

"So you're just a regular, run-of-the-mill burglar? You weren't here earlier, tossing rocks?"

"Rocks? No."

Maintaining his hold on Earl's arm, Riley came to his feet and hauled the other man upright. Earl tried to jerk away, but only managed to cause himself more pain. "Buck, check his pockets."

Earl kicked and fought, prompting Riley to add a little more pressure. The man's back bowed with a rank curse.

Ethan showed up then. He looked far more disgruntled and angry than Riley. "What the hell are you doing, Riley?"

Buck dug in the man's pockets and produced a pack of cigarettes, loose change, and a knife. "Sorry, Riley, no wallet, no I.D."

"Shake out a cigarette."

Buck sent him a look. "It's a hell of a time to start smoking." He smacked the pack until one cigarette emerged, saying to Earl, "Nasty habit, bud. Smoking can kill you."

Earl tried to kick out at Buck and with little effort, Riley forced him to his knees.

Ethan crossed his arms over his chest. "The cops are here. Should you be abusing him that way?"

"Since he keeps fighting me, he's lucky I don't tear him to pieces."

As luck would have it, Dermot and Lanny rounded the corner. They stiffened when they caught the occupants of the scene. "Christ almighty, Riley. What the hell is going on?"

Riley forced the big man flat again, put a knee between his shoulder blades and said to Dermot, "Give me some cuffs."

Dermot rolled his eyes, but did as told. After the restraints were in place, Riley did a quick search of his captive, but found no other weapons. He released Earl into Lanny's legal hands. "Read him his rights."

"I know my job, Riley. You want to tell me what the hell we're arresting him for?"

"Sure thing. He was in Red's apartment when I showed up." Riley handed Lanny the cigarettes. "And he smokes the same brand I found on the ground below her balcony."

"Well, I'll be damned. What'd he do inside? Did he steal anything?"

Indicating the contents of his pockets, which Buck still held, Riley said, "That's all he had on him, and I don't think the blade is Red's, so it must be his own. You can add concealed weapon to illegal entry. I think we interrupted things, but I've yet to have a look around inside. You can go on. I'll be down to the station in a little while." Then Riley thought to add, "Hang on to him, okay?"

Dermot grinned. "Judge Ryder is on a fishing trip, not due back till Monday. I'd say it's a safe bet we'll have him till then."

Lanny and Dermot each took an arm while Lanny started the familiar litany on rights. They led Earl to the cruiser. Riley watched, still tensed, until the big man was folded into the back seat and the door securely closed.

Then he became aware of the silence around him. He looked at Harris, who had his brows raised, Buck who grinned and Ethan who stared at Riley so long, Riley finally said, "What?"

"You're a regular savage, Riley, you know that?"

Riley shoved his way past his friend. "Screw you, Ethan."

Ethan laughed. Buck stepped up and drew Riley to a halt so he could squeeze his biceps. "Pure steel," he crowed to his friends. "Like a real-life action hero, he is."

Harris tucked his hands beneath his chin and said in a falsetto voice, "My hero."

Grumbling under his breath, Riley jerked free and went to the balcony. Damned idiots. When he jumped up and grabbed the railing, all three of his foolish friends started joking again. Riley did his best to ignore them as he swung a leg up and pulled himself over the railing. He noticed Ethan, Harris and Buck followed suit, climbing the balcony rather than taking the long walk around the complex to the front door.

Several neighbors were out, watching the proceedings with great curiosity. Once he'd regained his feet, Riley waved down to them. "A minor break-in folks."

They looked skeptical.

Of course, Buck was still scaling the balcony and Harris had only one leg caught awkwardly over the top rail. Riley shook his head and went inside. When Ethan started to follow, Riley warned him off. "Stay put a minute, okay? I want to have a look around. There's less chance of anything being disturbed if it's just me."

"If you need anything, give a yell."

Riley went to the bedroom first. He knew better than to tamper with evidence or disrupt a crime scene, but this wouldn't be the first time he'd ignored his conscience to do what he thought was best.

In this case, they weren't dealing with a death. More important, Red's feelings were at stake.

If anything would embarrass her, he wanted to know about it and, if possible, spare her. His intentions were altruistic—as unselfish as they'd been the first time he'd broken his own code of honor.

He saw right off that her dresser drawers had been dumped. Lacy panties and bras littered the floor in haphazard disarray, looking like a flock of fallen butterflies. Her pajamas and T-shirts had also been dumped.

Everything from her dresser top had been shoved to the floor, including hair combs, jewelry and perfume. Items from her closet had been sloppily rearranged and her bedding pulled apart.

What really caught Riley's eye, though, were the damn rubbers tossed everywhere. Dragging a hand over his face, Riley considered the situation, but he gave in before he had time to really think it through. Rushing, he gathered up the condoms and stuffed them into his pockets. He had more than one reason for doing so.

If his friends saw them, they might think they were his and the teasing would be endless, considering the size of the damn things. In fact, he intended to dispose of them posthaste so he didn't get caught with them in his pockets. It would give him a reputation he'd never live down.

But the biggest reason was that Red would be appalled if anyone knew she had them. Obviously, they had nothing to do with whatever Earl—if that was even his real name, which Riley doubted—was looking for.

Her nightstand drawers were now empty. Riley looked around the carnage, but didn't see the photo of Welling or the damn books anywhere. Earl hadn't had them on him, and what would he want with them anyway? That had to mean that Red had taken them with her.

He didn't mind the books—hell, he'd be happy to read them with her. But the last thing he wanted in his home was Xavier Welling's smiling face. Especially since he knew Red saw the man as some sort of paragon of goodness, a damned representation of what men should be. If she expected him to measure up to a precisely staged public persona, she was sure to be let down.

Ethan said, "Everything okay, Riley?"

With the condoms out of sight, Riley called back, "Yeah. You can come in."

Ethan entered the room, followed by Harris and Buck. "Damn, someone is definitely looking for something."

Harris stared toward her underwear. Using only his pinkie, he lifted a teeny tiny thong of shimmery pale pink. "I thought redheads weren't supposed to wear pink."

Riley grabbed the garment from him and stuffed it in his pocket—with the condoms. Hell, it was hard enough for him picturing Red in the sexy bottoms. He'd be damned if he wanted Harris doing the same.

Buck propped his hands on his hips. "Do we clean this up or leave it?"

Riley shook his head. "I have a camera in my truck. I'll take some photos then we'll tidy up before Regina sees it. It'd only upset her."

Ethan crossed his arms over his chest. "All things considered, I want to give Rosie a call. We're going to be a while and I want to make sure she's okay."

"Tell her to get a list of groceries from Regina. I'll stop at the store on my way home."

Harris grinned. "Why, don't you just sound so domesticated?" He started to reach for a satin demibra, and Buck grabbed his arm, but he was laughing, too.

"Leave the unmentionables to Riley before he twists your arm behind your neck."

Riley glared at them both before heading out to his truck, but his thoughts soon left his goofy friends. He had a man in custody. He had Red in his apartment.

Things were moving right along.

REGINA HEARD the front door opening and her heart shot into her throat. Jumping to her feet, she ran to greet Riley.

With his tongue hanging out, Butch kept pace, pretending they were in a race. She knew it was idiotic, knew that Ethan said Riley was fine, but she wanted to see him for herself, to be sure.

He'd just stepped inside the door, awkwardly holding his keys in one hand while juggling grocery bags with his other. Regina halted in front of him.

Riley glanced at her in surprise. "Hey, what's wrong?"

A little embarrassed but still anxious, Regina blurted, "I was worried."

His gaze lingered on her face, his mouth curled. "About me?"

"Yes. And don't be insulted. I know you can take care of yourself."

"And you still worried?"

She nodded, which made his expression warm all the more.

Without looking away from her, Riley kicked the door shut and shifted both bags into one arm. Reaching out, he snagged her close and his mouth brushed hers. "Thanks, Red. But you don't need to fret, okay?"

She sighed. He sounded like the idea was unheard of. "You aren't invincible, Riley. And Ethan called and told Rosie what happened and—"

"And I'm fine." He gave her a squeeze. His hand started down her back toward her bottom, then he looked beyond her. His hand stopped at the base of her spine and he nodded. "Hey, Rosie. Ethan's right behind me."

"I figured as much." She sauntered forward, grinning. "So, hero, how you doing?"

Riley rolled his eyes and allowed Regina to take one of the bags. Suddenly Butch let out a demanding, yodeling howl, and when Riley looked down at him, he came up on his hind legs, dancing in excitement.

"Well, what a greeting." Riley lifted the little dog to eye level. "Met at the door by a beautiful woman and a faithful Chihuahua. What more could a man ask for?"

Regina wanted to smack him. "Riley, please tell me you didn't tackle some maniac who broke into my apartment."

He winked and, still holding Butch close, walked around her to the kitchen. She looked at Rosie, who shrugged, then she stalked after him. "*Riley.*"

"Yes, dear." He was in the kitchen, Butch over his shoulder while he unloaded groceries one-handed. "Since you cooked last night, I'll do the deed tonight.

Steaks on the grill or spaghetti? They're my two specialties, my only specialties really, so I bought both. Or we can go simple and just have sandwiches. What's your pleasure?"

Regina held on to her temper by a thin thread. She was in his house, and he wanted to help her. She drew a breath. "Do you or do you not have a man in custody?"

"Yeah, we do. Thing is, the bastard isn't talking. We don't even have his name yet. But, luckily, Judge Ryder is out fishing."

Regina shook her head in confusion. "So?"

"So this is a small town, not the big city. Things are done differently here. Ryder's been around forever because no one cares to run against him. Because of that, he feels comfortable taking off for days at a time when the weather looks right to catch a big bass." He winked at her. "The weather looks right."

"What does some judge fishing have to do with the guy who broke in?"

"He can't be arraigned until the judge comes back. That gives us more time to check him out. I have a gut feeling that once we turn him loose on bail, he'll disappear."

Nervousness made her voice tremble. She clasped her hands together tightly, trying to calm herself. "What are you holding him for?"

"Illegal entry and concealed weapon for starters. He ransacked your bedroom, honey, but he didn't steal anything and nothing was really damaged."

The ramifications hit her. "So he was looking for something."

"I'd say so. Whatever it is, he hadn't found it before we interrupted." Riley gave Butch an absent pat as he moved from the cabinet to the refrigerator. "The guys helped me clean up the mess."

The guys. Aware of Rosie lounging in the doorway, Regina eased closer. Her heart slammed in her chest and her palms were damp. "He, uh, trashed my bedroom?"

Riley turned toward her. After a long look, he leaned down and whispered near her ear, "Hey, it's all right, babe. I confiscated the rubbers before anyone could see."

Her relief was overwhelming. "Thank you."

His grin gave her fair warning. "Harris gathered up your panties. Sexy stuff." His gaze dipped down her body. "Makes me wonder what you're wearing right now."

Rosie cleared her throat. "It's rude to whisper in front of guests."

Riley straightened with a sigh. "Since when are *you* a guest?" He glanced at his watch in a show of impatience. "Shouldn't Ethan be here by now?"

"Trying to get rid of me?" Rosie laughed. "And here I was ready to vote for steaks."

Riley looked pained, which mirrored how Regina felt. She wanted to be alone with him, to ask him details on what had happened.

Ethan sauntered in. "Soon as I get everything out of the truck, I'm taking you home, woman."

Rosie turned to drape her arms around his neck. "Really? What for?"

It was Ethan's turn to whisper, Rosie's turn to blush. In a rush, she said, "I'll help you unload."

It was another half hour before Regina was finally able to corner Riley and get some answers.

Not once had Butch left his side. He'd followed Riley to the truck time and again, then around the apartment, watching while Riley helped to put her things away in various places. He hooked up her computer in the room he'd given her to use as an office. It was a guest bedroom, but Regina knew Riley didn't want her using the bed.

With everything now in place, they sat on the back patio so Butch could run the length of the lead Riley had stretched between two trees. Regina stared at Riley, on the edge of her seat.

"What if he'd had a gun, Riley? What if he'd pulled that knife on you?"

Sprawled out on a chaise, his ankles crossed, Riley laid a forearm over his eyes to shield them from the late-afternoon sun. "If the dumb son of a bitch had dared to pull a knife on me, I'd have..." Belatedly, he lifted his arm to take in Regina's expression of horror. His frown smoothed out. "I'd have disarmed him, honey. Okay?"

She couldn't bear the thought of him being in danger because of her. "Are you really that good?"

He sat up and swung his legs around to face her. Treating her to a somber, very direct stare, he took her hands and said, "Yeah."

He'd answered without boasting, just matter-of-factly stating what he saw as a truth. Regina shook her head at such confidence.

"Later," he told her while giving her hands a squeeze, "I'm going to show you how good I am."

Oh, the way he said that. His low tone and sensual smile left her uncertain to his meaning. Cautiously, she asked, "You are?"

"Might as well get started on your training, don't you think?"

Well heck, so *that's* how he meant it. Disappointment warred with common sense. Still, private self-defense lessons wouldn't be at all the same as what they'd done in his gym. There, he'd been all business, politely distant, and a true gentleman given the other onlookers. Here, they'd be wrapped in privacy. The thought of being alone with Riley, feeling his body over hers, touching in all the most sexual places, made her breathless. "I suppose."

"So much enthusiasm." He pulled her off her seat and into his lap—something he never would have done in his gym. She thought he might kiss her, and truthfully, she wanted him to. In the short time he'd been at her apartment and then at the station, she'd missed him. She'd worried about him, too.

Instead he said, "Tell me the name of the guy who harassed you at work, and that ass you were engaged to."

"Why?" She tried to twist around to see him, but he hugged her closer so she could barely move. The fact that she was thinking about intimacy, and he apparently wasn't, left her flustered.

"I'm going to talk to them both. And no, don't argue, Red. I won't embarrass you. You have my promise on that."

It wasn't Riley she worried about. He'd already proven to have her best interests in mind. But her ex-fiancé… "I don't know what you think they can add to the equation."

Riley shrugged. "Maybe nothing. But it can't hurt to ask them a few pertinent questions, now can it?"

Actually, it could probably hurt her pride a lot. She bit her lip, but finally nodded. Riley was a professional who knew his business inside and out. It would be ridiculous to contradict him. "The man I worked with is Carl Edmond. He's a nice enough guy, just different. Sort of intense."

"Intense how?"

"Not in a bad way. Just overzealous about everything, his work, his life—"

"And you?"

She couldn't deny that. "For a while, maybe. He fixated on me. He told me he loved me, but I knew that wasn't true. His courtship became a bother before he wised up, but he was never threatening."

Riley didn't seem convinced. "And the other guy?"

Regina hated to talk about him. She couldn't mention his name without memories swamping her, leaving her hollowed out with humiliation.

But this time, seated on Riley's lap, held in his arms, it was easier. "His name is Luther Finley." She closed her eyes and prayed Luther wouldn't reveal anything of their private past to Riley. Not that Luther considered anything private. She'd found that out too late. "I assume Carl still works at the paper. He loves his job a lot. And Luther should be in the insurance building across the street. He's a salesman." She drew a breath. "Want me to write the names down for you?"

"Carl Edmond and Luther Finley. I won't forget." Riley rubbed his big hand up her arm, then down again. He was silent, introspective, and yet he kept touching her as if he couldn't help himself.

When his thoughts finally turned from the men, Regina felt the shift in his mood and she wanted to rejoice. She tipped up her face—and Riley accommodated her by capturing her mouth for a long, deep kiss. She felt the drumming of his heart, tasted the damp warmth of his mouth, and didn't want him ever to stop.

With his mouth still touching hers, he murmured, "Damn, you taste good."

He tasted better than good. Delicious. Regina pressed closer to slip her tongue into his mouth, deepening the kiss again and making Riley groan in response.

The warm sun beat down on them, cooled only by the gentle breeze. Riley's strength wrapped around her, giving the illusion that nothing bad could ever happen. From his wide chest and thick shoulders to his flat abdomen and strong thighs, he was all male. Being with him, alone each night, would make it nearly impossible to keep any emotional distance.

Had it been only a day ago that she thought she needed to know him better before becoming involved?

She knew the truth now. Already she was way too involved, and knowing him better only made it worse. Riley believed in her when no one else did. He put himself in danger for her. By his own admission and by the evidence of his actions, he was more than capable of handling any threatening situation. On every level, he fascinated her.

She was already half in love with him.

Riley's hand moved up alongside her face. His big thumb stroked her cheekbone as he lifted his mouth. "I want to ask you something, Red."

Regina felt herself floating. She smiled. "Hmm?"

"Why did you bring the books and photo here?"

Her sensual haze lifted. She opened her eyes to see Riley watching her, his expression probing, filled with command. Because their noses practically touched, it was a rather intimidating stare.

"C'mon, Red, tell me." She started to straighten, but he shook his head. "No, I like you like this. I enjoy holding you."

"Oh." She shifted a little to get more comfortable, felt his erection, heard his low groan and immediately stilled. No one had ever touched her as much as Riley did. Not even her fiancé had wanted to hold her this way. "I brought the books because I thought, well, we are going to be staying here together. I'm not an idiot. I realize what we'll likely do before too long."

The heat in his blue eyes darkened. "Today." His kiss was soft, gentle. "It's going to happen today."

Such a sensual promise shattered all other thought. She could only stare at him.

"But, honey, you don't need a book."

Brought back to the reality of the moment, she winced and gave an awful admission. "I think...maybe I do."

Without seeming to move, he gathered her closer to

his body. He glanced out into the yard at Butch, saw he was sprawled out in the sweet grass in a spot of bright sunshine. Then he looked to make certain they were well hidden between the sections of privacy fence that lined his small patio.

His gaze came back to her, resting first on her eyes, then her mouth. "How can you need a book when everything you do makes me hot? You dress up all classy and it makes me think about stripping you naked. I catch you in worn pajamas and I want to feel how soft and warm you are under them. You cook dinner and I obsess about the way your bottom sways while you stir the food."

She'd been listening with fascinated wonder until the last, then a startled laugh broke free. "You do not."

"I do." And in a growl he added, "Your backside has played prominently in all my most recent fantasies." He punctuated that statement by grasping her firmly in both hands, giving her behind an affectionate, caressing squeeze. "Damn. I can't wait to get you naked so I can explore it in more detail."

Her face flamed. "Riley."

"Regina." His smile touched her heart. "I especially like the charming way you blush. Hell, everything about you makes me hot. Believe me, honey, getting you into bed is the objective. Once we're there, it doesn't matter what you do. I won't be complaining."

Hearing him say it made her almost believe. Had she allowed Luther's spiteful comments to influence her too much? It had been such a difficult time, such a humiliation.

But Riley wouldn't lie to her, she knew. He was better than that. "All right, I'll forget about the books if you promise to tell me what you like."

He drew her marginally closer. "I like you."

"You know what I mean."

He pressed his face into her neck and gave a gruff laugh. "The way you keep talking about this, like it's going to happen any second now, has me close to exploding."

Regina thought it *was* going to happen at any moment. She frowned at him, but before she could tell him that she wanted him now, he said, "There're a few things I want to clear up before we get sidetracked."

Sidetracked? Is that what he called making love with her? Feeling put out by his blasted patience, she said, "Like what?"

He leaned away. Some of the teasing laughter in his eyes darkened to a more serious emotion. "The photo. And why the hell you brought it along."

7

BLESS BUTCH'S LITTLE HEART. He choose that moment to interrupt with a loud spate of barking. Regina sat up to see that a rather hefty golden retriever had come over to check him out. Regina started to jump up in alarm, but Riley stayed her with a hand on her arm.

"That's Blaze. She's a sweet dog, honey. She won't hurt him."

Regina doubted that after she saw Butch try to sprinkle the gorgeous creature's nose. Yet rather than snap at him, Blaze lunged back playfully, shook her head, and ran the length of his lead so that Butch could chase her.

He went so fast trying to keep up, he tripped over his own nose and managed a complete somersault without stopping. When he ran out of rope, he yelped, and Blaze trotted back to him.

Regina laughed. "I think Butch is in love."

Riley sat up behind her, his arms looped around her waist. "Poor bastard. I wonder if she'll keep pictures of other dogs around just to make him nuts."

Regina turned sharply to stare at him. Was he jealous over the picture? But no, that would be too absurd. Senator Welling represented strong values, not sexual allure. Surely, Riley understood that.

Riley lifted her away and came to his feet. The dogs

were still playing, making a terrible racket that didn't bother Regina at all. She couldn't keep her eyes off Riley as he stretched, then looked up at the blazing sun.

In the next instant he reached for the hem of his shirt and pulled it off over his head.

Regina didn't so much as blink. His upper body was gorgeous. Dark hair liberally covered his well-defined chest. Sleek, prominent muscles in his shoulders bunched and moved as he haphazardly folded the shirt and laid it over the back of her chair. In unself-conscious masculine display, he dragged one hand through his chest hair, scratching a little, then flexed his shoulder and rotated his head.

Regina's mouth went dry. In something of a rasp, she asked, "What are you doing?"

"It's warm out here." He glanced down at her. "And I'm a little stiff from jumping off your damn balcony so many times." So saying, he turned to head inside and Regina caught sight of a bruise on his ribs.

"Riley." She was out of her chair in a flash, catching his arm and holding him still. "What happened?"

He looked down at the darkening flesh she indicated. "Nothing. That must be where I hit the ground when I tripped him. I had no idea there were so many little stones everywhere."

Wishing she could soothe him, even heal him, her fingertips grazed over his warm skin. "I'm sorry."

His gaze stayed on her face, piercing and bright. "No problem, Red." He unsnapped his slacks.

Regina stepped back in a rush.

"I'm going to go change before we have our little chat about that picture. Be back in a second."

Change? As in, change into *what?* Less clothes? It was bad enough when he was at the gym wearing shorts, T-shirt, socks and athletic shoes. But at the gym, there was always a crowd around, plenty of people to keep the situation less intimate.

Here, there was no one. And she just knew if Riley started flaunting himself, she'd end up the aggressor.

He was only gone a minute, but it was long enough for Regina to give herself a hot flash, thinking of the night to come.

"You getting hungry, Red?"

She jerked around, then took an automatic step toward him. Good Lord, the man oozed sex appeal. He wore gray low-slung drawstring shorts, and nothing else. She realized she'd never seen his feet before. They were big, sprinkled with golden brown hair, narrow, and as sexy as the rest of him. Right now, braced apart as they were, he seemed to have planted himself firmly against opposition. Hers?

Not likely. Not when everything about him appealed to her.

Slowly, Regina allowed her attention to climb upward, taking in every inch of his body. Muscular, very hairy calves, nice knees. *Incredible* thighs.

Her heart raced. She already knew firsthand how strong his thighs were. She'd watched Riley grappling with some very big bruisers at his gym and he always dominated. Swallowing, she looked higher still and saw the hem of his shorts, hanging to midthigh.

A little higher and she saw... Oh my. Regina blew out a breath that sounded part whistle, part exclamation, and not in the least ladylike. Under normal circumstances, she would have been appalled at herself. But the soft cotton molded to his sex. He was right, small condoms would never fit him.

Breathing became more difficult. As an intelligent, educated and modern woman, and as one who had recently read some informed books on the subject, she knew size didn't matter. That hadn't been her problem with Luther at all.

So why did it feel like a volcano of heat had exploded inside her?

As she stared at him, unable to draw her gaze away, something twitched. Her brows lifted. Fascinated, she watched as Riley became semierect. She put a hand to her throat.

Riley, blast him, never moved.

Deciding it might be safer to continue on with her visual journey rather than keep staring at him *there,* Regina looked at his hard abdomen. That didn't help one iota. The hair around his navel and the silky trail below it appeared soft, tempting her to touch it. She wanted to so badly, but would that be crossing the line?

At the moment, did she care? How could any woman remain rational when faced with such provocation?

Almost from the start, she'd wanted Riley. Every day the feeling grew stronger. Other than her acute sense of caution and propriety, there were no real reasons for waiting.

She moved toward him.

Riley made a gruff sound of expectation.

Savoring the moment, she put her hands on his

sides, luxuriating in the feel of hot smooth skin drawn taut over firm muscle. Experimentally, Regina caressed him, her thumbs inward to trace over the sleek muscles slanting toward his groin.

She looked at his face. He was rigid, flushed, waiting. "I want to touch you, Riley."

"Do."

One simple word that somehow sounded so provocative. When she looked again, she saw that he now had a full erection. *Very* full. Just from her touching his waist? Intrigued, she asked, "You like this?"

"Yeah." He drawled out the word, husky and deep.

Emboldened, she slid her hands around his back near the very bottom of his spine, close to his sexy muscled tush. The position brought her closer to his chest and she inhaled deeply. "You smell so good, Riley."

He leaned forward, pressed his mouth to her temple, and whispered, "Is that really where you want to touch me, Red?"

Her nose brushed his soft chest hair when she shook her head. She liked that, so she did it again. "No."

"I didn't think so."

Deciding to try pure honestly, she said, "We're outside...."

"No one can see us."

"But still..."

"I'm a man, not a schoolboy. I can control myself. Nothing happens unless you say so. Feel free to touch all you want and to stop when you want."

Her heart expanded. Such an incredibly generous offer.

Such an incredibly generous man.

She tipped her face up. "Will you kiss me while I do it?"

His expression hardened and his voice went low and rough. "My pleasure, baby."

This kiss felt different. Regina hadn't realized he'd been holding back, that there were so many nuances to kissing until that moment when she felt all his carnal intent in the way he devoured her mouth. It was an eating kiss, hot and hard and overwhelming. He would make love to her now—she understood that and reveled in the reality.

Again and again, his tongue sank past her parted lips and into her mouth, stroking seductively. She felt consumed. That was enough of a distraction that Riley had to nudge himself forward into her belly to remind her of what she wanted, of what *he* wanted.

Bringing her hands around, she first toyed with his navel. His abdomen had grown rigid, the muscles clearly defined, growing more so as she touched him until he felt like granite with no give to his flesh at all. The hair there was just as silky as she'd imagined.

Breathing hard, her awareness suspended, she encountered the waistband of his shorts, the ultrasoft cotton material and finally the long, solid length of his penis.

They both groaned.

Riley's fingers tightened and he lifted his mouth away to gulp for air. Keeping his forehead against hers, he encouraged her by saying, "That's it. Damn, Red..." And he groaned again, harsh and broken.

Regina could have spent an hour just exploring him. On so many levels, he fascinated her, the freedom he allowed, his open response. Her fingertips trailed up his length, measuring him, then back down again— and she felt the shuddering response of his body.

Driven by curiosity, she cupped beneath his shaft, cradling his heavy testicles in her palm and heard him hiss in a breath.

"Easy." His long fingers gripped her upper arms.

"Like this?"

"Yeah." His grip loosened, caressed, encouraged.

They spoke in muted whispers, hers awed, his raw with arousal.

Suddenly he kissed her again, so ravenously that she forgot what she was doing and her hands left him to grasp his neck, holding tight. Strong arms enclosed her, stealing her breath. Her lips were swollen, her head spinning, when Riley again cupped her face to place sweet little pecks on her chin, her cheeks, her forehead.

"You know what I think, Red?"

Overwhelmed, she whispered, "What?"

"That turnabout is fair play."

Her stomach jumped and her heart began a wild race. When she got her eyes open, Riley was smiling at her.

"You'll love having me touch you, Red. I promise. But for right now, we should take this indoors before things get out of hand and neither one of us makes a clearheaded decision."

Her head would never be clear again.

Riley nodded in the direction of the yard. "Butch fell asleep with his new lady friend."

A safer topic if ever there was one. Regina turned

and saw that Blaze had stretched out on her side in the thick grass. Her golden fur looked beautiful with the sun glinting off it. Butch was curled up on her neck, his whole head practically in her ear. They made such an adorable picture, Regina's heart nearly melted and stupidly, tears filled her eyes.

"Tonight," Riley whispered to her, "I want to sleep with you curled that close." He didn't give her a chance to reply to that, not that she had a reply anyway. He picked her up and started into the house.

"Butch..."

"Will enjoy his freedom in the yard. I'll leave the window open. Don't fret, honey. We'll hear him if he needs us." Riley walked right past the room he'd given to her and into his own bedroom.

When he reached the bed, he went down with her in his arms. She'd known of his strength, but still he amazed her. He treated her weight as negligible, arranging her as easily as he would a pillow. Straightening away, balanced on one arm, he said, "You're wearing entirely too many clothes, Red. What'd you say we take them all off?" And before she could find her voice, he already had her sleeveless sweater up and over her head.

RILEY KNEW if he gave her too much time to consider things, she'd decide it wasn't proper to be having sex with him in the middle of the afternoon with the window open. He was done giving her time. She now felt comfortable touching him sexually, and he knew, even if she didn't, that they had a future together.

The rest would fall into place.

The second her sweater cleared her head, he reached for the clasp to her bra. He heard her gasping breaths, felt the urgent bite of her nails in his upper arms.

The bra, bless her feminine little heart, was white lace and so damn sexy he could have spent an hour just appreciating the way it decorated her small breasts. Instead, he flicked the front clasp open, pulled the thin cups apart, and visually sated himself.

"Beautiful."

Regina made a sound of startled embarrassment and covered herself with her hands.

Riley forced his gaze from her white breasts to her face. "Harris was wrong. Pink and red go real nice together."

Her embarrassment faded behind confusion. "What are you talking about?"

A long curl of titian hair had come loose, and Riley used it like a feather to tease the side of her breast. "Red hair and pink nipples. It's a sexy combination."

"Oh." More color exploded in her cheeks. "But what does Harris have to do with—"

No way would Riley tell her about Harris picking up her pink panties. "And this pretty blush." He put his mouth to her cheek and felt the heat of her flush. "You're beautiful, Regina, and I don't want you to be embarrassed with me."

He gently caught her wrists, aware of the fragile bones, how small she felt in his big hands. Drawing her arms up, he pressed her hands firmly to the mattress at either side of her head. He released her and her breasts shivered with her nervous, jerky breaths.

"But I—"

Her protest died on a gasp when Riley leaned down and took one soft, plump nipple into his mouth. Regina's back arched and her fingers threaded through his hair.

Holding her shoulders down on the bed, he sucked gently, keeping the pressure light, using his tongue to tease her nipple into a stiff little point. When he lifted his head, Regina had her eyes squeezed shut, her bottom lip caught in her teeth and her body held tight.

"You like that, honey?"

Without opening her eyes, she bobbed her head.

Riley smiled, then looked at her body. Her upper torso was so slim, her rib cage narrow and her breasts pert. He skimmed his palm down her side, then inward to the clasp of her slacks. "I want you naked. I want to see all of you."

Her eyes flew open.

"Once you're naked, I can get naked and think how good that's going to feel."

Her lips parted. "Yes."

Gently, he pried her fingers from his hair and again raised her arms over her head. "I love seeing you like this, Red, stretched out on my bed." He studied her from top to toes, then kissed her belly. "Now don't move."

She agreed by curling her fingers into the bedding, holding on tight.

Her sandals slipped off easily enough, but Riley took the time to kiss each arch, then each ankle. There was one spot just behind the ankle bone that when pinched, could cause agonizing pain, maybe even paralyze the limb. In the same regard, a featherlight touch sent thousands of acute nerve endings on alert. Riley tickled with his tongue, soothed with soft kisses.

She had sexy legs, long and sleek. Her casual white slacks unbuttoned with ease, and building the anticipation, he slowly drew down the zipper. Her belly hollowed out with her sharply indrawn breath.

Riley spread his fingers wide over her hips and dragged the pants down to her knees. Her panties were the same lace as her bra, showing the springy auburn curls over her mound. He wanted her so badly he hurt, but he didn't want to rush her, he didn't want her to start searching for her damn books.

Using one fingertip, Riley traced the triangle of pubic hair. He couldn't wait to taste her, to have her completely naked and open....

"Riley?"

"Yeah?"

A long heavy silence filled the air before she said, "I don't think I can take all this waiting. My patience isn't as strong as yours."

Riley looked up at her face. Her hands were fisted, her pupils dilated, lips parted.

"Just a little longer."

Her pants tangled around her ankles with her trying to kick them off and Riley had to finish that chore for her. Her panties came off next, and then she was beautifully bare.

Her aroused scent filled his head. He kissed her belly, each hipbone, an inner thigh. Alternately, he made the kisses gentle, then rough, sometimes laving with his tongue, sometimes nipping with his teeth. Regina squirmed and gasped, on edge, unsure what the next touch would bring. He could feel the urgency pounding through her.

Parting her legs, he licked the joint of her thigh and groin, where her skin was ultrasmooth and delicate.

"Riley, please..."

Regardless of what she said, she couldn't be ready yet. His mouth open and his kisses deliberately damp, Riley made his way back up her body. She grabbed him, kissing him hard, while his hands covered both her breasts. Her nipples were tight now, her breasts swollen. He caught her nipples and rolled, squeezed, tugged.

She pulled her mouth away. "Riley."

"Shh." He kissed her again, silencing her protests while continuing to torment her nipples. The more aroused she got, the more she'd enjoy his caresses. Her legs shifted restlessly, moving alongside his until he stilled them with one of his own. Caught under him, Regina could barely move, and that suited Riley just fine.

Keeping her legs trapped, he leaned up to look at her face. "I want you as ready as I am, Red."

"I am," she all but wailed.

"No." Smiling, he dragged his callused fingertips over her ribs, her belly and finally between her thighs. The crisp curls were damp, her lips puffy, sleek with moisture. His breath caught. "Well now, maybe you are." He pressed his middle finger inside, just past her swollen flesh, no deeper. She was most sensitive here, at her opening, so he used that knowledge to circle, dip, circle again. He relished her broken moan, the way her body tried to move with him.

"I should... I should be doing something."

"What is it you want to do?"

"Touch you."

His control nearly slipped. "No, not yet. I'm on the ragged edge as it is."

Her eyes opened and her head lifted off the pillow to shout into his face, "Then quit playing around!"

Riley almost laughed. Regina amused him so much, even at a time when laughter should have been eons away. "All right. Tell me how you like this."

Her head dropped back with a groan as he began moving his finger deeply in and out, making her wetter still. As he did so, he kissed his way down her body. The closer he got to her sex, the more she stiffened.

"Riley?"

"Hush." He nudged her thighs farther apart, took a moment to enjoy her scent, breathing deep, then with a groan, he covered her with his mouth.

She gave a small cry, arching hard.

At the first flick of his tongue, her body clamped down on his finger. He licked, stroked, and finally, catching her small clitoris carefully with his teeth, he suckled.

Her body strained away from him, but Riley held her hips, keeping her still. He loved the feel of her voluptuous bottom in his hands, the taste of her on his tongue, the hot, wild sounds she made. As her excitement peaked, he worked in another finger, stretching her, filling her. She lifted up to meet his mouth, grinding against him, so close.

When he knew she was ready to come, he sat up and snagged a condom from the nightstand. Regina cried out in protest at the delay, and the second he got the protection taken care of, she opened her arms to him.

Riley settled between her wide-open thighs. Wanting every possible connection, he held her face to kiss her and nudged his way inside. She was tight, but so wet he knew he wouldn't hurt her. With one hard thrust, he entered her completely and Regina lifted her legs to wrap around his waist. He found a rhythm that quickly had them both straining toward a climax.

Her mouth devoured his, biting his bottom lip, sucking on his tongue. He loved it.

He loved *her*. If only he could make her understand that.

Sweating, his heart thundering in his chest, he slid one hand under her behind to tilt her hips up so he could enter her more deeply. That was all it took. She started coming with broken groans and mewling cries and that pushed Riley right over the edge. He could feel the throbbing clench and release of her body on his cock, the frantic bite of her nails on his shoulders, the way she shuddered and writhed under him.

He pressed his face into her neck and growled out her name. Regina wasn't quite so restrained. She screamed.

Two seconds after Riley's body went utterly limp and he gave Regina his weight, Butch began barking hysterically.

He felt Regina stiffen, but he patted her hip and made the manly offering. "I'll go get him."

Her hands slid off his back to land limply on the bed. "Thanks."

Riley forced himself to his elbows to see her face.

Her eyes were closed, her French braid ruined, her makeup smudged. She was sweaty, just as he'd predicted.

And, thank God, she was finally his.

RILEY ATTEMPTED to wake her with a kiss to her forehead. Regina moaned, rolled to the side and slept on.

They'd spent the night making love and apparently, Regina wasn't used to such excesses. Truthfully, neither was he.

It had surprised him how often he'd wanted her. Watching her eat a simple dinner in her robe, seeing her coddle the silly little dog, catching her secret smiles and sudden blushes, had all provoked him. He hadn't been able to keep his hands off her.

And she hadn't minded in the least.

It'd been tricky, getting Butch to leave the room without kicking up a fuss. Riley figured he'd need to stock up on toys and tasty chews to distract the dog.

After her fourth release, she'd conked out and hadn't really come to since. Once he'd realized she was done for, he'd worked her pajamas back onto her then let Butch in the room. She hadn't protested when the dog burrowed under the covers, or when Riley had pulled her close and held her all night long.

She hadn't even awakened.

It drove home to Riley just how exhausted she'd been, and the toll her worries must have taken on her.

He hoped his presence would ease those worries, because, from now on, she'd damn well be with him. Beyond that, he didn't know if his lauded control extended to sleeping chastely each night, even if they'd made love prior to going to bed.

He hated to disturb her now, but he didn't want to leave for the day without saying goodbye. Butch seemed just as determined to keep him from doing so.

He and the dog had been up for an hour and more than once Butch had whined at her door, apparently wanting Regina to join them. Now that he was back in the bed with her, he dashed from Regina's feet to her head and back again, trying to protect all of her—from Riley.

Riley lifted the miniscule dog. "I may have gone overboard last night, bud, but I don't accost women in their sleep."

Regina's eyes fluttered open. "Riley?"

At the sound of her soft, sleepy voice, some insidious warmth expanded in his chest. "After last night, were you really expecting another man to wake you up?"

He saw confusion flit over her face, then realization. She snatched the sheet over her head. "What in the world are you doing in here?"

He sat on the bed beside her, causing a dip in the mattress. Her rump rolled into his hip. "I slept here. It's my bed, remember?"

She groaned.

"And because Butch wanted under the covers, I put your pajamas back on you, so you don't need to hide."

"It's not that," she mumbled from under the covers.

Ah, Riley thought, appearances again. Silly woman. "Do you have any idea how sexy you look all rumpled and warm?"

She went very still. "I do?"

"Yeah. Makes me want to strip naked and get back into bed with you." He gave a grievous sigh. "But unfortunately I have some stuff to do, so I only wanted to wake you so I could say goodbye."

One slender hand emerged from the blankets, shooing him away. "I'll be out in a second."

Smiling, Riley patted her hip and stood. As an enticement, he said, "I have coffee ready and waiting."

She made a rumbling sound of appreciation. "I'll be right there."

Ten minutes later she emerged with her hair brushed and pulled back in a ponytail, wearing a casual green sundress. Her eyes were still puffy and there was a crease in her cheek probably formed from a pillowcase.

Riley wanted to consume her. Again. Last night hadn't even taken the edge off his hunger. He didn't think a hundred years could do that.

As he watched, she made her way unsteadily toward the table. "Riley? I suppose I should admit that I'm not at my best in the morning." She ended that with an enormous and inelegant yawn, giving proof to her statement.

"Coffee will help. You sit and I'll pour it for you."

She plopped down in the chair. "Thank you."

The dog made a beeline for Regina. She roused herself enough to lift him into her lap and treat him to several kisses to his round head.

Riley could have used a few of those kisses. Not that he was jealous of the attention she gave Butch, and not that he didn't understand how sluggish she felt. But this was the proverbial morning after and she'd barely looked at him.

Then he decided *what the hell*.

He handed her a mug of coffee, but forestalled her from tasting it by leaning down and taking her mouth in a warm morning kiss. "Now that," Riley said as he straightened, "is the *proper* way to say hello after a night of satisfying debauchery."

Regina gave him a bemused look, snatched up her cup and swilled her coffee. There was no other word for it. In two long gulps, her mug was empty. Enjoying this side of her, Riley fixed her another cup then seated himself across from her.

"You do remember last night, don't you?"

Her eyes darted away from his. "Of course I do. No woman in her right mind would forget a night with you. Especially not a night like that."

"Thanks. I wanted verification, given the way you passed out on me."

She groaned and covered her face with one hand. "I'm sorry."

Riley reached across the table and took her slender wrist. Her skin was warm, smooth. "I'm not. You needed the sleep."

"That's no excuse for rudeness."

Riley nearly choked on his laugh. "You were not rude, I was excessive. And believe me, I have no complaints."

"But..."

"*None*, Red. Okay?"

Her expression softened. "I don't have any complaints either. In fact, I think I owe you a few compliments."

Riley grinned with her. "You can give them to me tonight."

"Why tonight?" She looked more awake now and somewhat interested. "I thought maybe we could..."

He groaned. "Don't tempt me, Red. Nothing would please me more than hauling your sexy butt back to bed. But I'll be gone till this afternoon."

Her disappointment was plain to see, filling Riley with satisfaction. "I thought you were on vacation."

"I am, but I want to talk to your two swains, Carl and Luther, then stop by the station and see how things are going with our intruder."

Her brows pulled down. "I'm not at all sure I like this idea."

"Why?"

"Don't look so suspicious, Riley. I'm not hiding anything important."

That clarification *important* rang like a bell in his head. "So you're hiding unimportant stuff?"

"No! And don't twist my words. It's just that I'm sure neither Carl nor Luther has anything to do with my trouble."

"With this type of continued harassment, it's almost always someone you know, and more often than that, it's someone you've been romantically involved with." She quit her protests to groan instead. Riley laced his fingers in hers. "Now, don't take this the wrong way, but I'd like you to promise me you won't take off anywhere while I'm gone."

She rubbed her eyes tiredly. "I have nowhere to go. In fact," she said, giving him a direct look, "I thought I'd finish up my article on the talent show. Once that's done, I can start on your interview."

He didn't want to talk about the damn interview right now. While he intended to discover everything he could about Regina, he detested the thought of her prying into his past. He came to his feet and stepped around the table to reach her. Caging her in with one hand on the seat and the other on the back of her chair, Riley said, "We've got a lot to do today, sweetheart."

She stared at his mouth. "We do?"

He nodded. "We're going to start on your private lessons today, remember?"

"Oh."

Seeing her disappointment almost had him laughing out loud. Aware of Butch's low growls, he touched her nose. "I'll make sure you enjoy them, okay?"

Her eyes darkened. "Okay."

"Tonight is the ceremony at the Historical Society. They're honoring Senator Welling." He watched her face and added, "I thought maybe we could go."

Excitement brightened her eyes and added a smile. "You mean it?"

Now he was jealous. Welling represented her ideal man, and for most, his stature was as unattainable as the moon. "It won't be a social call, honey. I want a chance to talk to your senator, and this seems like it might be the best opportunity."

Her excitement remained plain to see. "He's not just my senator, and Riley, you'll like him a lot, I know it."

Riley would have liked the guy more if Regina weren't so infatuated with him. "If he cooperates with me, I'll have no complaints."

"I really don't think he'll have anything to share, but it'll be good to see him again."

Because he didn't want to hear her talk about Welling, Riley kissed her quick and hard. He felt Butch nipping at his chin, his ear, doing all he could to scare Riley off. Riley drew back to stare at the little dog. "Where's your toy?"

Butch's ears shot up. He maneuvered down Regina's leg to the floor and took off at a dead run for the hallway. He returned with the stuffed Chihuahua in his mouth and dropped it at Riley's feet.

Riley laughed. "Smart dog. All right, I can play for just a few minutes, but that's all." And to Regina he added, "Finish up your coffee. There's cereal in the cabinet, fruit in the fridge. Help yourself, okay?"

Her expression was tender when she nodded. "Thanks."

Ten minutes later, Riley was on the floor, the stuffed toy caught in his teeth while he and Butch indulged in a feigned tug of war. Butch gave it his all, jerking and growling in his attempt to tear the toy away from Riley. Riley growled back, a stuffed tail and leg caught in his mouth.

Regina laughed. "You're both nuts."

Riley straightened. "Now he knows how to grapple. Did you see his triceps? Or would they be triceps, considering dogs don't have arms?" Riley shook his head. "Either way, he's buff and built like a lean bulldog."

Butch took off in a flash, dragging the toy, but when Riley didn't pursue him he returned only to smack Riley's ankle with it. "No," he told Butch. "I gotta go. Get Regina to play."

Butch dutifully dragged the toy to Regina. She laughed. "Gee, thanks."

Riley tipped up her chin to give her a long, thorough kiss. "If you need anything while I'm gone, just call me on my cell phone."

He knew he had to leave before he decided not to go at all. Today he was going to get some answers. The sooner the better. Then he'd come home to Regina.

Soon he'd have everything worked out.

8

THE SECOND Riley was out the door, Regina made plans. She called Rosie at work first to find out Ethan's and Harris's schedule. She didn't want to call either of their homes if there was a chance she'd wake them. As firefighters, their hours varied. Regina told her they were both on second shift that week, and that Ethan, at least, should be up and about.

She called him and made an appointment for him to visit her at Riley's house. Next, she called Buck and left him a message since he didn't pick up.

Finally she chanced a call to Harris. A woman answered, temporarily throwing Regina off. "Um, is Harris around?"

"Who is this?" the woman asked with heavy suspicion.

Regina was about to reply when she heard some grumbling in the background, then Harris's voice on the phone. "Hello?"

"It's Regina. I'm so sorry I'm interrupting."

"No, you're not." That statement caused another ruckus in the background. Harris covered the phone, did some grousing, then came back to ask, "What's up? Everything okay?"

"Oh, yes. I just... I'm going to be doing an interview on Riley and since he's gone for most of the afternoon and he doesn't want me to leave his apartment, I figured I could start by talking to his closest friends. Ethan's coming over in a few minutes, and I hoped, if you weren't too busy, maybe you could come by after him."

She heard the amusement in Harris's voice when he asked, "Does Riley know you're inviting us over?"

"No, why?"

Now he laughed outright. "No reason. None at all. And yes, I'd love to come over. Hell, I wouldn't miss this for the world. Want me to pick up Buck and drag him along? You can kill two birds with one stone."

"I already called him. He's working."

"He's the boss. If he can't take off for a few hours, who can?"

Regina laughed. "No, that's okay. I'd rather talk to each of you one on one."

Harris snickered. "Really? All right then." He laughed again. "This is going to be fun." He hung up before Regina could ask him what he meant.

RILEY MADE IT to Cincinnati in a little less than an hour. It was easy enough to find the newspaper building. He thought about going in to talk to Carl first, but changed his mind and parked in the lot for the insurance company. At the lobby desk, he asked about seeing Luther, and was told to go to the fourth floor.

On the elevator ride up, Riley thought about what he'd say. He realized he wanted Regina's ex beau to be guilty, just for the satisfaction of cleaning the guy out of her past. If she did have any residual feelings for him, finding out he was the one harassing her, with nothing but hurt feelings to motivate him, ought to take care of it.

There was no one at the receptionist's desk. Riley glanced at his wristwatch, saw it was lunchtime and waited only a moment before mentally saying, *To hell with it.* He strode to Luther's door, raised his hand to knock—and got a whiff of sickeningly sweet smoke. Pot.

What the hell?

He tried the door, but it was locked. After knocking sharply, he called out, "Luther Finley?"

There was a lot of shuffling movement behind the door before it finally opened. A man close to Riley's height, with straight black hair and shrewd blue eyes, stood there. His suit was immaculate, expensive and in good taste.

He made a great appearance. Shit. First the senator, and now this clown. If Regina was drawn to *GQ* men, Riley didn't stand a chance.

"Yeah? Who are you? What do you want?"

So this was the man Regina had bought sex books for? This was the man she'd hoped to please in bed?

Riley wanted to punch him in the nose. The urge to do so made it difficult to breathe. Ruthlessly, Riley brought himself under control. He would not behave like a Yeti. He would not prove himself to be a jealous fool.

Looking beyond Luther, Riley saw an open window, a desk drawer slightly ajar. Perfect. If he couldn't hit him, he could at least have the upper hand. There must be a fairy godmother sitting on his shoulder, to be given this advantage.

"Can I help you?" Luther said with strained impatience.

"You Luther Finley?" At the other man's nod, Riley flashed a badge. "I'm Riley Moore, with the Chester Police department. I need a moment of your time."

Luther's eyes opened wide and he reeled back two steps. "The police? What the hell did I do?"

"I want to ask you about an acquaintance of yours. Understand, Mr. Finley, this is an informal visit and you're not in any trouble. Yet. I'd just like some information."

Riley saw the moment the man relaxed, wrongfully assuming he'd ignore the pot. "Yeah? About who?"

"Regina Foxworth. She seems to have gotten herself into a bit of trouble."

The look of curiosity faded beneath a smarmy smile. "Regina is in trouble?" He actually laughed. "Yeah, sure. Come on in and pull up a chair. I'm glad to help."

And Riley thought to himself, *I just bet you are.*

REGINA HANDED Ethan a tall, icy glass of cola. "Now, tell me what you know about Riley."

Ethan looked more wary by the second. He glanced around the obviously empty apartment and said yet again, "I'm not sure this is a good idea, Regina."

"No, it's okay. Riley gave me permission to interview him. And he didn't want me to leave the apartment, so this is a good compromise. He won't mind."

"Uh-huh." Ethan sipped his drink, still undecided. "What exactly do you want to know?"

Regina studied Ethan while she considered what to ask him first. He was a very attractive man with his dark blond hair and deep, intelligent brown eyes. As a firefighter he was, by necessity, built almost as handsomely as Riley. But she'd never had any interest in Ethan. No, she'd seen Riley and been lost. She'd fought her reaction to him, but fighting did her no good. Last night had proven that.

She sighed. "Has Riley had any recent romantic involvement?"

Ethan choked, stared at her, and choked some more. She got up to thwack him on the back, but Butch didn't like that and started to howl. For some unknown reason, he'd taken a real dislike to Ethan.

Gasping and wheezing, Ethan waved her away. Regina resettled herself, allowing Butch to skulk back into her lap with a surly look thrown toward Ethan.

"Well?"

"What does that have to do with your interview?"

In the primmest tone she could muster, Regina lied, "His social habits will be of interest to everyone reading the article. They'll want to know about *him*, not just his work."

Ethan didn't look convinced. He drew a deep breath, cast her another suspicious look, and finally murmured, "He dates. Not seriously, not often."

"Really?" Now that was interesting, considering the amount of energy Buck and Harris apparently put into tomcatting around. And from all accounts, Ethan had been worse before Rosie brought him to his senses. "So he's selective?"

Ethan frowned over that. "I have no idea. It's just that Riley is...different. He's not like most guys I know.

He thinks differently and he sees the world differently."

"He's dangerous."

Slowly, Ethan nodded. "I suppose you could say that, but only to someone on the wrong side of the law. To most people he's an advocate, a defender. Riley uses all his skill to help protect people." Ethan settled back in his seat, a little more at ease. "If you could have seen how he took that guy down—the one he found in your apartment—it was something else. Riley didn't look winded, didn't look like he'd used much effort, and he didn't look like he had a speck of emotion in him. Cold, swift and effective. One second the guy was running and the next he was completely immobilized by Riley. It was both awesome and a little unsettling." Then, more to himself than to Regina, Ethan murmured, "It still amazes me that he left the SWAT team to come here."

"Why did he? Do you have any idea?"

"Not a clue. Riley only lets people in so far. I'd trust him with my life and I know he's one of the best men around. But his past is off-limits. Not once in the five years I've known him has he given so much as a single clue."

Disappointed, Regina let out a long breath. Trying not to be too obvious, she asked, "Who has he been seeing most recently?"

Ethan rolled his eyes. "You."

"No, I mean before I moved in here."

"You."

"But we didn't..."

"Date? Doesn't matter." Ethan gave her a warm

smile. "I remember we were all at Rosie's for dinner the day after we first met you. Riley talked about you—"

"Saying what?"

Ethan shrugged. "It wasn't what he said so much as how he said it. We all knew right then that he was interested. And the day of the fire..."

Ethan grew silent, stiff. He couldn't talk about that awful day without looking a little green. He closed his eyes, took two shallow breaths, and swallowed. "As distracted as I was that day with Rosie, I noticed how Riley staked a claim."

Regina pulled back. "He did *what?*"

Grinning, Ethan nodded. "He laid claim to you."

Flushing a little with umbrage—and with pleasure—Regina said, "But that's ridiculous."

"What did you think it meant when he picked you up and didn't put you down?"

"My head was bleeding. I was dazed."

"And unable to walk?" Ethan snorted. "He held you because he wanted to and because he decided you were his. Any guy within seeing distance knew it, and because Riley is who he is, they paid heed."

"But he hasn't asked me out or in any way acted interested." Ethan raised a brow and she quickly amended, "Until recently, I mean."

"Baloney. He's tried to teach you how to defend yourself and he's been following you around, keeping an eye on you, making your welfare his business. And he stares at you, Regina. Cracks Harris and Buck up, just to watch the way he watches you." Ethan smiled at that. So did Regina. "Riley's not one to spill his guts, but if I had to guess, I'd say you are a major distraction."

And then what? "You really think so?" She hated sounding so hopeful, but if Riley cared a little for her, if what he felt was more than just sexual...well, that would change everything.

"I know so." Ethan glanced at his watch, then stood. "Sorry to rush off, but Rosie has a few hours free." His grin told Regina all she needed to know. They loved each other so much. She wanted what they had, the closeness, the caring.

If she could have that with Riley, it'd be more than she'd ever dared to hope for.

RILEY PACED around the desk to the open window. "So you and Regina were engaged?"

Luther snorted. "Is that what she told you?"

Stiffening, Riley kept his back to the other man and asked softly, "Are you saying she lied?"

He snickered. "No. She *thought* we were engaged. But you know how it is. Regina's one of those women who has to have everything right and proper. She'd never have let me in her bed without a ring on her finger."

The clawing need to break the bastard's nose nearly choked Riley. "I see. So *you* lied?"

"I told her what she needed to hear. If you've met her, then you'll understand. She's so ladylike on the outside, I thought maybe she'd be a wildcat in bed. That made the deception worthwhile, or so I thought. But she was still stiff as a broom. No satisfaction at all. It was like sleeping with a damn board." He gave a hoarse laugh. "What the hell does this have to do with the trouble she's in?"

Riley turned to Luther with a cold smile. "Someone is bothering her. Damaging her property, scaring her. I'm trying to figure out who."

Luther shot to his feet. "You're accusing *me?*"

"Just gathering the facts—though it certainly sounds like you have a store of animosity for her."

"No. Hell no. You can stop gathering right now. When we split, I said good riddance to the little prude."

"No regrets, huh?"

Luther grunted. "Hardly." He took two incautious steps toward Riley. "You know what that twit had the nerve to do?"

Riley cocked a brow, but Luther didn't wait for him to reply. "She bought some goddamned books on sex, and she actually wanted to talk to me about them. She acted like I held part of the responsibility for her lack of enjoyment in the sack. I told her it was damned tough to satisfy a cold fish. She got pissed, and whenever she got that way, she got all stiff and righteous with her haughty little nose in the air."

Riley's smile hurt. "Yes, I know what you mean."

"You've seen it, haven't you?" Again, Luther didn't wait for a reply. He nodded, then chuckled. "Well, I was sick and tired of her acting superior so I told her it'd help if she'd try a little harder to get my interest. She's so damn skinny, I suggested a boob job." Here he laughed outright, even slapping his knee.

Riley churned with anger, but not by so much as the

flicker of an eyelash did he let Luther know. "She's slight, but I haven't noticed her lacking at all."

"Then you haven't seen her naked. She's got a nice ass, but the upstairs leaves a lot to be desired."

Riley went mute with rage. It was bad enough that Regina's childhood had instilled in her a need to make a good impression, but then to have this jerk tear her down and make her think her best wasn't good enough....

Luther's grin lingered. "Man, she hit the roof. She got all red-faced and told me she wouldn't marry a man who didn't want her as she is."

Satisfaction swelled inside Riley. *Bravo, sweetheart*, he silently congratulated her. Then through his teeth, he asked, "That ended the engagement?"

"Blew it to smithereens, which was more than fine by me. She tossed my ring back at me, walked away and I haven't seen her since. I haven't *wanted* to see her since." He leaned back on his desk and crossed his arms. "You know what? I bet she rubbed some other poor bastard the wrong way and he's retaliating. It'd serve the little witch right to get hassled a bit. Maybe it'll get her to loosen up and live a little."

Riley figured Regina would loosen up when the right man loved her, namely him. With trust would come complete comfort. But until then, he couldn't let Luther get away with insulting her.

He rubbed his chin thoughtfully, then moved forward half a step. Very calmly, giving Luther no warning, he said, "Let me explain something to you." Without haste, he reached for Luther's upper arm, clasped him in his right hand, easily found a pressure point, and applied the right grip to make the man's knees buckle and to force a short screech of pain from him.

Eyes wide with fear and teeth gritted in pain, Luther literally hung in Riley's one-handed grip.

Without compassion, Riley watched him writhe in agony. In a voice more deadly because of its softness, he said, "Regina Foxworth is mine. Eventually I'll marry her. Anyone who insults her insults me."

Luther let out a long broken groan. "You didn't tell me that. Hey, I'm sorry!"

Riley shook his head. "No, not good enough. You see, how do I know that you won't go spreading these nasty rumors about her to other people? I think I should impress on you exactly what I'll do if I ever hear of you even mentioning her name again."

Luther gasped. "Please..."

Riley released him.

Slowly, holding his numb arm, Luther straightened. His face was pale with lingering agony.

Legs braced apart, hands on his hips, Riley said, "You have a lot more pressure points, Luther, places that when manipulated just right, can cause pain you can't even imagine. How many do I need to demonstrate before you fully understand?"

"One's enough. I swear."

Riley said, "I don't know..."

Luther rushed behind his desk, which gave him a false sense of safety. His arm hanging limp and useless, he managed to stand more or less upright. "You better get out of here," he groused in a shaky voice. "You're a policeman. You can't do this to me. I'll report you—"

Riley pulled open his desk drawer. "Yeah? Well, I

can haul you in for smoking dope on the job." He lifted out a joint, along with a small bag of marijuana. "What do you think your supervisors will say to that?"

Luther's eyes went wide.

"I'll only say this once, Luther, so pay attention. Stay away from Regina, keep your foul mouth shut, and what you do on the job is your business. I really couldn't care less."

Luther slumped, but then another voice intruded from the doorway. "I care."

Riley looked up to see a slender woman in her mid-thirties, dressed much as Regina often did in business-casual wear, staring at Luther with hatred.

"You're the receptionist?" Riley asked.

Her chin went up another notch. "And I was his fiancée." She pulled off a miniscule diamond ring and pinged it off Luther's forehead. "Not anymore."

Luther groaned.

Riley went around the desk to the woman. "You overheard?"

"Yes. All of it. I came back to my desk a few minutes ago and I eavesdropped."

Riley felt a little uncomfortable. "I should apologize..."

"No. He's a pig and I'm sorry if he hurt your girlfriend at all."

"He hasn't. Regina is too smart to be hurt by him." At least, Riley hoped that was true. He'd find out for sure tonight—*after* he got her naked and let her know in no uncertain terms that he thought her utterly beautiful. Anything she didn't have, she didn't need.

The receptionist's shoulders went back. "What you

did to him...the way you barely touched him yet he started whining in pain. How did that work?''

''Why?''

''I think it might be a useful thing to know.''

Grinning, Riley fished a business card out of his wallet and handed it to her. ''If you ever get over to Chester, stop into my gym and I'll teach you.''

''Thank you.''

As he left the insurance building, Riley admitted to himself that it probably wasn't Luther bothering Regina now. He'd watched the man's every expression and had seen only weakness, conceit and lewd innuendo. No real deception. Riley would keep an eye on him, but he doubted anything would turn up.

Once outside, he stopped on the sidewalk to stare at the newspaper building across the street.

One down, two to go.

REGINA GRINNED at the determined way Buck tried to make friends with Butch. Buck looked like a felled titan in his black T-shirt and worn jeans, stretched out on the floor on his stomach, his chin on his crossed hands, meeting the dog at eye level.

Butch didn't cooperate.

No matter how softly Buck spoke to him or how he cajoled, the dog continued to give a low, vibrating growl of warning.

Buck glanced up at Regina, his green eyes alight with mischief. ''You sure this damn dog isn't part badger?''

''I don't understand it. He's always so sweet to me.''

Buck came to his feet, ruffled Regina's hair fondly

and said, "Well now, honey, you're very easy to be sweet to."

Half-embarrassed by that odd praise, Regina gave an uncertain smile. "Um, thank you. If you'd like to take a seat, I can get you something to drink."

"No thanks. Let's get right to it. You want the scoop on Riley, right?"

"Well, yes." But she rushed to explain, "I'm doing an interview on him."

"Uh-huh." Buck stretched out his massive arms along the back of the sofa and grinned. "He's hung up on you big-time. Never thought to see the mighty Riley with a weakness, but damn if he isn't acting smitten. It's downright fun to watch."

Regina blinked, then blinked some more. "Oh, but I didn't mean to—"

"What? Find out how he feels about you? Course you did." Buck continued to grin. "I don't mind. Riley's tough, no way around that. But any man who guards his past that closely has a few serious wounds. I'd like to see him happy and I happen to think you can accomplish that. So whatever I can do to nudge things along, count me in."

Such an awesome outpouring, from *Buck* no less, left Regina momentarily distracted and without a single coherent thought in her head. "Uh..."

"I think some woman did him wrong, don't you?"

Regina stared. "Well, I..."

"That'd make sense, huh? If it was a guy, Riley would have just kicked his ass, not quit his job and moved away. And now here you are, putting him into a possessive lather, helping him to focus on better things. I'm glad you moved in with him. Ought to keep him occupied." He winked.

Regina went hot to the roots of her red hair.

"So." Buck slapped enormous hands on his thick thighs. "Is that all you wanted?"

She cleared her throat twice and attempted to get control of the situation. "I, uh, had hoped to learn more about Riley's job, what he does, his training...."

Shaking his head, Buck came to his feet. "Sorry. I don't know anything about that. He used to be SWAT, but left the city to come here. Since Chester has no need of a SWAT team, Riley fell back on his old training of CSI. That's the beginning and end of what I know." Then he frowned. "Well, one other thing."

"Yes?"

He pushed up his T-shirt sleeve over a massive, bulging shoulder and flexed his arm to show off a seriously impressive biceps muscle. "See that?"

"Yes." Regina knew she wouldn't be able to circle that muscle even if she used both hands. "It'd be rather hard to miss."

Buck nodded. "I'm strong. I do a lot of physical work, day in and day out at the lumberyard. Men walk a wide path around me if I'm annoyed. But I don't have a single doubt in my mind that Riley, scrawny as he is, would make mincemeat out of me if he ever had a notion to."

He smiled as he made that claim, especially the ridiculous part about Riley being scrawny. Compared to

Buck, he was certainly leaner, but scrawny? Nope, not by anyone's standards.

Buck tugged his sleeve back down and nodded. "That's some serious training that goes beyond what you're taught for a job, even if that job is SWAT. It's a lifestyle, a personality, an inherent part of the man. Riley's like a warrior born in the wrong century. He'd die to protect those people he cares about, and he'd expect loyalty in return."

Was this Buck's idea of a warning for his friend? Regina didn't know for sure, but she touched the arm he'd just bared and offered a smile. "I would never do anything to hurt him."

Buck patted her hand. "I know. That's why I think you're perfect for him."

He started for the door, and both Regina and Butch followed. "You know, Buck, I'm a little surprised. You're usually so quiet."

"Naw. It's just that with Harris around, who can get a word in edgewise?" He laughed, opened the door, and there stood Harris with his hand raised to knock. "Well, speak of the devil."

RILEY EYED the tall, thin fellow with the wire-rimmed glasses and neatly combed blond hair. He wore a suit, complete with a tie and jacket. Everyone else in the room had removed their coats and rolled up their shirt-sleeves, loosened their ties. Not Carl Edmond.

The outward attention to detail had probably appealed to Regina, even if the man hadn't.

Bent close to the keyboard, a slight frown on his

brow, Carl typed industriously at the computer. Riley snagged a chair and pulled it up close. Carl was so absorbed in his task, he didn't notice Riley until he sat down.

Shifting around, first startled, then polite, Carl asked, "May I help you?"

"Carl Edmond, right?"

"That's correct."

He didn't look alarmed, only curious. He didn't look like a predator either, but Riley had learned long ago that even the most innocent expression could hide deceit. It was a lesson he'd never forgotten. After discreetly flashing his badge, Riley said, "I'm here informally, just to ask a few questions if you're willing."

Looking around the crowded room with a slight blush, Carl said, "Perhaps we should go someplace more private?"

"Sure."

Riley allowed himself to be led into an employee lounge. There was no one else present. Carl glanced at him. "Would you like some coffee?"

"Please." He was so courteous, Riley wondered that Regina hadn't been taken with him. He reminded Riley of a masculine version of Regina. Carl set a steaming cup of coffee in front of Riley, along with a small square napkin.

With those courtesies taken care of, Riley said, "You know Regina Foxworth."

Carl had just started to sip his coffee, but he stopped, face alight with pleasure. "Yes, yes I do." And then with sudden concern, he added, "She's all right, isn't she?"

"She's fine. But someone has made her a target." Riley explained the things that had happened, all the while watching Carl Edmond for the slightest flicker of guilt.

There was none.

"But this is terrible. Regina is... Well, she's a gentle, beautiful person. I don't mean her looks...well, her looks, too. But she's one of the kindest women I know. I owe her a lot. If there's any way I can help you to find this evil person..."

Riley leaned back in exasperation. Carl had a touch of melodrama. "Why do you say you owe her?"

The man actually blushed. "Well, it's a long story, and I really hate to admit it, but I fancied myself in love with her. I'm afraid I made a real nuisance of myself, too, following her around like a lovesick pup." Here he shook his head and chuckled. "But Regina remained kind. She sat me down, explained that she only cared about me as a friend, and then she suggested that I wise up and pay more notice to the bagel girl."

"The bagel girl?"

"She delivers fresh bagels to this room twice a day. I didn't understand at first, but I did as Regina suggested." He held up a hand, showing off the gold wedding band. "Thanks to her, I'm now married to Carolyn. It was love at first sight, at least for me."

Riley ran a hand through his hair. "Great. Congratulations." And another dead end. If the new wedding hadn't been enough, Carl's obvious happiness would have swayed Riley. He pulled out a card and pushed it across the table toward Carl. "If you think of anyone who might want to hassle Regina, would you give me a call?"

"I'd be glad to." When Riley stood, Carl reached out and caught his arm. "Mr. Moore? Please. Take good care of her, okay? She's a very, very special person."

Riley nodded. "You have my word."

9

HE HEARD the raucous noise even before he finished unlocking the door. Music, laughter, playful barking.

Brows drawn, Riley turned the knob and silently pushed the door open. No one noticed him.

Regina sat cross-legged on the floor, her back to the sofa where Harris lounged on his side, his head propped up on a fist. Butch ran up Red's body, over her shoulder, along Harris's length, then back down over Regina.

Her shoulders were touching his stomach.

Harris's nose was practically in her ear.

Riley closed the door with a resounding click that seemed more effective than a hard slam. Butch jerked up. His small furry face went blank with surprise, then lit up with blinding pleasure. Yapping with berserk glee, he tumbled off Harris, rolled over Regina and came charging toward Riley. Ears bouncing and little paws moving with lightning speed, he reached Riley and slid to a halt.

"Well, hello to you, too, squirt." Riley lifted him up and got his face thoroughly bathed with a warm doggy tongue. All the while he stared at Harris.

Slowly, his mouth twisted as if to hide a grin, Harris straightened. "Hey, Riley."

Riley continued to stare.

Regina scurried to the stereo and turned it off. Hands behind her back, she smiled shyly at Riley. *Shyly?* Now what was she up to?

She hesitated a second, then with only a bit less enthusiasm than Butch had shown, she came to him, went on tiptoe and kissed him. Not a polite welcome peck. Nope. She cupped his face and moved her soft sweet lips over his until Riley forgot that Harris was behind her. He snagged an arm around her waist, hauled her up against him, and pressed his tongue past her parted lips. When she went limp against him, Riley reluctantly ended the kiss.

"You're home," she said in a breathless whisper.

"Earlier than you expected?"

Harris chuckled. "Gee, Riley, is that a gun in your pocket or are you glad to see...Regina?"

Regina gasped, her thoughts plain on her face, but Riley relieved her mind by saying, "It's a chew toy for the dog."

Regina looked down at his lap and blinked at the ludicrously large bulge there. "Oh."

Harris cleared his throat. "I think I'll take this as my cue to get lost."

He had the nerve to stop at Regina's side, kiss her cheek, and then wink at Riley. When Riley narrowed his eyes, Harris laughed and held up both hands. "Don't hurt me, Riley, okay?"

Riley rolled his eyes. "What are you doing here?"

"Ah, well, I'm just one in a long line of guys who've trooped through your door today."

Regina elbowed him hard. Riley took her arm and pulled her to his side so she wouldn't hurt herself poking at Harris. Regina was red in the face, Butch was squirming to be petted and Harris was trying to sidle out the door.

Riley opened it for him. "Later, Harris."

"Right." With a fast salute, Harris took off.

Riley closed and locked the door, then, ignoring Regina for the moment, headed to the couch with Butch. "So, my man, you missed me?" He seated himself and Butch immediately climbed up on his chest to sniff his face. He barked, bit Riley's chin and then tried to dig underneath his shirt.

Laughing, Riley set him aside. "Anxious for your gift, huh?"

Regina inched over to the couch. She smiled. "You're spoiling him, Riley."

"I thought it might keep him occupied while I carried you off to bed."

He heard her gasp, but didn't comment on it. He was so wired, so damned...*needy* after talking to the other men, he knew if he didn't have her soon, he'd explode. He pulled a large rawhide bone out of his pocket. Butch's eyes widened and his ears came forward in an alert pose.

Setting the bone on the floor, Riley asked, "Think you can handle that?"

The dog ran down Riley's leg and circled the bone, examining it from every angle, making both Regina and Riley laugh.

"It's bigger than he is."

Butch got one corner in his mouth and started backing up with the bone until he was completely hidden beneath a side table.

"That ought to keep him busy." Riley stood and turned toward Regina. "Now for you."

Regina chewed her lower lip. "Yes?"

"I missed you."

Her smile quivered the tiniest bit. "I missed you, too."

Riley slipped his arms around her waist. Staring down at her, he said, "I was going to go really slow, Red. I was going to start by teaching you a few self-defense moves, because that's important. Then I was going to carry you to bed."

"You've been teaching me self-defense moves for a while now," she reminded him.

"Not alone. Not in private where I can mix the lessons with kissing and touching."

"You've changed your mind about teaching me?"

"No, I just don't think I can wait. We'll work on your lessons afterward."

Her smile was sweet, sensual and teasing. "I'm glad. I've been thinking about you all day, too. I don't want to wait."

She caught her breath when Riley lifted her into his arms. He strode into his bedroom, pushed the door quietly shut with his foot, and sat on the edge of the mattress with her in his lap. "How could you have been thinking about me when you had Harris here entertaining you?"

She pushed his jacket off his shoulders. Riley helped, moving his arms until the coat fell to the bed. Next she began undoing his buttons. "We talked about you."

"You did?" He didn't like the sound of that, but with

her small cool hands now on his chest, he found it hard to concentrate.

"Yes." She bent and kissed his throat. "I wanted to start your interview by talking to your friends."

Riley stiffened, but she caught his neck and quickly kissed him, scattering his thoughts.

"They respect you a lot, Riley."

"They?"

"Ethan, Buck and Harris."

His groan was due partly to dismay, partly to the way she removed his shirt and rained tiny kisses across his chest. "Hell, Red, you had all three of them here?"

"Mmm. They don't know any more about you than I do." She pushed him flat to the mattress, straddled his thighs and started on his belt buckle.

Riley settled his hands on her waist, charmed with her seduction, and so turned on he wanted her under him right this instant. "You know everything about me that you need to know."

She glanced up to give him a chastising smile. "No, I don't. But I can be patient. I've decided not to do the interview until you're comfortable talking to me about your past."

"Red..."

"Raise your hips." She had his slacks undone, so Riley did as ordered. She quickly skimmed them, along with his boxers, down his legs. She paused to tug off his shoes and socks, and then he was naked.

Regina let out a breath. "You are such a gorgeous man, Riley Moore."

"I'm glad you think so. Now come here."

"Just a second." She stood beside the bed and stared down at him. "You spoke with Luther?"

"Yeah. I spoke to him." *And I made him very sorry he ever hurt you.*

Regina nodded. She bent to pull off her sandals. "He, ah, told you about our breakup, didn't he?"

Rolling to his side so he could see her better, Riley propped himself up on one elbow. "He explained that he was an obnoxious blind ass who doesn't deserve you."

Her lips curled in a disbelieving smile. "Never in a million years would Luther say something like that."

"No, but that's the gist of it." Riley watched her fidget with the straps of her sundress. Would she be daring enough to lose the dress? He hoped so. "Whether he realized it or not, whether you realize it or not, you're an incredibly sexy woman, Red." With a grin, he added, "I sure as hell realized it the second I saw you."

He heard her inhale deeply. "Thank you." She reached for the hem and tugged her dress up and over her head. After tossing it aside, she pushed her panties down and stepped out of them. She straightened and waited.

It was the oddest feeling, Riley thought, shaking with lust while choking with tenderness. He'd never experienced it before, but then, as he'd just told her, he'd known from the beginning that she'd be different.

He reached for her and toppled her across his chest. He rolled, putting her beneath him, and cupped one satiny breast. "You're perfect."

"I'm—"

"Perfect." He looked up into her eyes. "I understand about hurt, Regina. People say and do things that, if we let them, can hurt us deep inside and linger for too damn many days and nights."

Her expression froze. "Someone hurt you?"

Riley decided then and there that he'd tell her. He wanted her trust, so perhaps he had to give it first. He wasn't a polished man and he didn't have the persona of the senator, but he could be honest. "My wife."

She went rigid beneath him. "You were married?"

"Yeah." Her naked body distracted him and he said in a growl, "Luther is an idiot. I wouldn't change a single thing about you." He bent and took a nipple into his mouth.

"Riley wait..." she said on a groan.

"Can't." He gently sucked while pressing his hand between her thighs. She was warm and soft, her springy curls already damp.

Regina waylaid him by catching his wrist. "Riley? There's something I always wanted to try."

Breathing hard, Riley forced himself to stop. It wasn't easy when he ached with the need for release. "What?"

"This." He let her push him to his back. Her breasts were against his chest, one of her legs between his. Her hair hung loose, silky soft and tousled. "Don't move."

He considered that a tall order considering the gorgeous view of her backside that she presented while twisting around to rummage in his nightstand for a condom.

Riley said, "In a hurry?"

"Yes. Tell me if I put this on you wrong." She

opened the small packet and bent close to his groin, intent on her task. He could feel her breath and it made him moan. She blinked at him in surprise. "I haven't even touched you yet."

"I know." It was a miracle he could string those two words together. Her hair tickled across his abdomen, his thighs.

She looked down at his cock and smiled. In the next instant, she had him in her small, soft hand, gently squeezing. "Is this what you want?"

His groan mixed with a laugh. "I want you any way I can have you."

"Would you like me to kiss you?"

His vision narrowed; every muscle in his body clenched. He said, "Yes," although he doubted she meant what he wanted her to mean. His body arched in delicious pleasure. "Oh God."

Her mouth was warm, damp, her tongue curious. Riley caught her head in his big hands and guided her, urging her to swallow more of him, raising his hips to help her with that.

Her small sound of wonder vibrated along his shaft, and his fingers clenched. He'd dreamed about this, about the prim Regina Foxworth giving him head— and enjoying it. The reality beat the fantasy all to hell and back.

For several minutes she drove him crazy, tasting, teasing, humming again. Finally, she lifted away and Riley's heart swelled at the evidence of her excitement. Her green eyes glowed with heat, her cheeks were flushed. "You taste good, Riley," she said in wonder.

Riley curled a hand around her thigh. He needed to come. He needed to be inside her. "So do you."

They stared at each other for a long moment before Regina bent to press one last innocent kiss to the head of his erection. Riley watched her straddle his thighs, saw her frown as she carefully rolled the condom on.

He checked it with her fascinated gaze never wavering, then pulled her over him. "Now what, babe?"

"Now I want to do it like this, with me on top."

"Yeah?" He gave her a crooked smile that almost hurt, he was so turned on. "I like that idea. That means I can see and touch all of you."

Her eyes darkened. "Yes." She lifted up, guided his cock to her opening, and slowly began sinking onto him. Riley held her thighs. She braced her hands on his chest.

It was incredible...seeing her face, watching her expressive eyes and the telling way her lips parted and her breasts rose with each deepened breath. "A little more," he urged, and her eyes closed as she wiggled, seating herself fully upon him.

Neither of them moved. Riley gasped for air, Regina's body clenched and relaxed around him.

"I can feel you throbbing."

He groaned and couldn't stop the lifting of his hips. Through his teeth, he growled, "I'm a nanosecond away from coming."

"Really?" She smiled down at him, then lifted.

"Really." She dropped and he said, "Regina..."

"I like this. Do you?"

Groaning again, he cupped her breasts, brushed her nipples with his thumbs, then caught them both in his fingers, lightly pinching, tugging. Her back arched, driving him even deeper.

He knew he wouldn't last so he moved one hand between her legs, gliding his middle finger along her swollen lips, taut around him, then up to her turgid clitoris. "Move, honey. Ride me."

Her fingers splayed over his chest and she began to rise and fall, faster and faster. He loved the small sounds she made, the way her face contorted with her concentration, her pleasure. Riley kept his fingers just where she needed them, treating her to a constant friction that worked with her own movements. Soon she was in the same shape as him, shaking, on the verge of exploding.

He brought his knees up to support her back and returned her thrusts, lifting her knees from the bed as he drove into her. With a startled cry, she collapsed against him. Her mouth opened on his shoulder, her teeth coming down in a tantalizing love bite.

The small pain pushed him over the edge. Riley lost control. He gripped her ass and pounded into her, groaning harshly with his own unending climax, the crushing waves of pleasure going on and on....

He wasn't sure how much time passed when he became aware of Butch jumping beside the bed, demanding attention. Regina was a soft sweaty weight over his heart.

"Hey?" He moved fistfuls of her hair aside, kissed her ear. "You okay?"

"Mmmrrmf."

Riley managed a grin. "What's that?"

"I'm fine," she said against his neck, wiggling lazily. "Better than fine. I feel extraordinary."

He stroked her behind. "Yes, you do."

Her giggle was one of the sweetest sounds he'd ever heard. She was totally relaxed with him. Soon, she'd love him—as much as he loved her.

"We have three problems. We're both sweaty and sticking together. The condom's going to become useless in about two seconds if we don't separate. And Butch is none too pleased to be ignored."

Regina pressed her face into his chest. "You smell good sweaty." Lifting up to see him, she asked, "Do I?"

Damn, but she wrenched at his heart. "Good enough to eat."

She smiled and blushed, then turned her attention to Butch. "You have to wait, sweetie. Give me a second to regain feeling in my legs, and I'll get up and play."

"That dog is worse than an infant."

"How would you know? Ever had an infant?" It was just an offhand remark, not really serious.

"No." Riley rolled her to his side, filling his hand with her hair so he could see her face. "I wanted a baby though."

That bald admission, especially after lovemaking, got her attention. "You did?"

"Yeah." He kissed her, then sat up in the bed. "Stay put. I'll be right back." He headed to the bathroom to dispose of the condom. It also gave him a moment to gather his thoughts and figure out how to say what he wanted her to know, to understand.

When he returned, she was sitting up against the

headboard, wearing his shirt and holding Butch. The dog took one look at Riley and tried to keep him out of the bed with his pseudo-attacks.

"You mangy little mutt, I'm the one who brought you the bone, remember?"

At the mention of the enormous chew, Butch's ears perked up and he went to the edge of the bed, whining to be let down. With a sigh, Regina lowered him to the floor. He ran out the bedroom door in a flash.

Riley found his boxers, pulled them on, and sat on the bed at her side. "You look good in my shirt."

She laughed, making a halfhearted effort to smooth her wild hair. "You know what I think? I think you just like giving compliments."

"Only to people who deserve them." He fingered the collar of the shirt, then undid the button between her breasts. He didn't know if he'd ever get enough of her—

Something solid and damp landed on his foot. Butch had dragged the colossal chew bone over to him, and was now jumping at the side of the bed again.

"Oh no. I don't want that thing in my bed."

A barked argument ensued. When Riley held firm, Butch got hold of the very edge of the bone and tried to stand up against the bed. He couldn't. He looked ridiculous with his mouth full and he made an odd snorting noise during his struggle. Riley couldn't help but laugh. "All right, you pathetic little beggar. You win. But keep it down at the foot of the bed."

He lifted both dog and bone, then laughed again when Butch did his best to hide the gigantic thing under the covers. Riley helped by lifting the blankets for him, then caught Regina's sweet indulgent expression. "What?"

She reached out and touched his jaw. "When I first met you, I knew you were very capable and strong. That's as noticeable as your blue eyes, and I told myself that I needed to get closer to you to learn some self-defense."

"Which you've yet to do."

She ignored that. "Then after a while I decided you were a terrific friend, too. You're so at ease with the guys and with Rosie. I wanted so badly to be a part of that."

"And you are."

"Yes." She touched his mouth, tracing his lower lip with her fingertips. "After I brought Butch home, I got to see how gentle you are. That was such a turn-on, Riley." Her smile trembled. "Now, seeing your patience and generosity, it occurs to me that you'd also make a wonderful father." She laughed. "Although you'd probably spoil your kids rotten."

Riley turned his head and kissed her palm. She was getting into some pretty deep stuff here. So far, she'd admitted to liking and admiring him. He wanted more. He wanted her love.

"I think we can spend a few minutes talking before we need to get dressed for the ceremony."

"I'd like to talk about...things."

"Yeah?" He moved into bed beside her, put his arm around her and tugged her into his side. "I haven't wanted to really talk to a woman in a long time."

"You prefer to just rush her into bed?"

He shrugged. "I haven't been a saint, but I haven't

been sexually attracted to that many women either. Now here you are, and I want to talk to you and be inside you at the same time. It's damn strange."

"Gee, thanks."

Riley hugged her. "You go first then."

He felt her nod before she said, "I always knew it wasn't me."

Riley just held her, waiting.

"I've never been ashamed of my build or thought I was lacking. I'm just me and I try really hard to be the best that I can. But even though I realized Luther is a creep, I was still...worried."

"Without reason. You're incredible, a beautiful person inside and out."

"Thank you."

Riley smiled at her continued good manners. "Any problems in the sack were his, Red. It was never about you."

"Yes, I know." She stroked his abdomen and sighed. "Especially now. After today, after being with you, I won't worry anymore." Then she turned into his side, wrapped her arms tight around him as if to protect him, and whispered, "But you didn't know, did you? The woman who hurt you—you blame yourself."

Riley tensed. "It's not the same thing, honey."

"Will you tell me what happened? Not for an interview and not for nosiness, but because I care about you, Riley. And I know from experience that it helps to talk."

A good start, Riley thought, then wondered if she'd feel the same when he finished his tale. "I've never told anyone before." He wanted her to know that, to understand the level of his trust. He shuddered at the small kiss she pressed to his chest, right over his heart. "She died, Red."

A strange stillness settled over her. "Your wife?"

"Yes." He was glad Regina kept her face tucked against him, rather than looking at him. He wasn't a coward, but he couldn't remember those awful days of lies and deceit—his and hers—without feeling raw. "She was having an affair with Phil, one of my friends from the SWAT team." With disgust he added, "A man I respected."

The silence felt heavy, almost suffocating Riley before she asked, "How do you know?"

Riley shook his head, once again wishing he could somehow change things. "I caught them in bed together. I came home from work early and found them in my bedroom, in my bed."

"I'm so sorry."

"I always have control, Regina. Always. But when I saw them, I didn't bother using it. I can't claim temporary insanity or a blinding jealous rage. That would be a lie. I was pissed off, completely furious, and I wanted to beat the hell out of Phil, so I did. I coldly, methodically, hurt him. Not permanently, but I did a lot of superficial damage."

"But listen to what you're saying. You could have killed him, Riley. You're more than capable. But you didn't. Instead you just hurt him, as he deserved."

Riley shook his head. "No one got what they deserved that awful day." He had to draw three breaths before he could continue. "My wife flew around me, screaming and crying. Phil... He was good, but he didn't stand a chance against me."

Regina fisted a hand on his chest. "He was in bed with your wife, Riley. Most men would react the way you did."

"Most men aren't me."

"Meaning you fight better than they could?"

He laughed. "There was no fight to it."

"And don't you see? Another man without your control might have killed him, even if he hadn't meant to."

He couldn't deny that. As a cop, he'd seen more than a few crimes of passion. "You know, it was strange, but a good part of my anger was for Phil's wife. She was seven months pregnant at the time."

Regina curled closer, both arms around him, one leg over his. Absently, Riley stroked her shoulder.

"God, Regina, when Phil finally left my house, my wife went with him and..." He hesitated, but she had a right to know. "They both died in a car wreck."

"They made their own decisions, Riley."

"They were both upset. Physically, Phil was in no condition to drive. I should have stopped them. I should have at least stopped her from going along. But I didn't." His throat hurt, but he said it all. "I wanted her out of my sight. I wanted her gone."

"But you didn't want her dead."

She sounded so sure of that. Many times, Riley had remembered that awful day and wondered. He'd been so detached through it all, as if his heart had been anesthetized. "No, I didn't want her dead." Saying it out loud made him finally believe it. He'd reacted, but without the intent of such dire consequences. "Hell, I didn't even want *him* dead. But when I got the call, I dunno, most of my concern was for Phil's wife. I kept seeing her in my mind, how happy she'd been, all the plans she'd been making for them as a family." He glanced down at Regina. "She was cute as hell pregnant and whenever we got together she'd show us the new baby clothes she'd bought or a bassinet or a toy."

"Oh God, how did she take the news about Phil and your wife...."

He shook his head. "I never told her, Red. Not about the cheating. I've never told anyone." He glanced down at her. "Except you."

Regina's eyes were big and soft, filled with understanding. "How did you explain them being in the car together?"

He laughed, but the sound wasn't humorous. "I was CSI—I knew how to cover my tracks. I made sure no one would know I'd been home when he and my wife left together, then I said my wife must have been helping him with a gift for the baby. I told everyone that they'd discussed it, made plans to buy something wonderful because Phil wanted to surprise his wife. No one doubted it. No one questioned me. Hell, no one even noticed my bloody knuckles." He swallowed down his own disgust. "They didn't see the bruises on Phil either. The wreck was pretty bad and the car caught on fire." His voice went so quiet, it was barely audible. "Neither of them was all that recognizable."

Riley could feel Regina shivering. "Was anyone else hurt in the wreck?"

"No, thank God. They went off the side of the road,

down into a gully. The car flipped and hit a tree. There were no other cars involved."

His stomach started churning; absently he rubbed it, trying to fight off the familiar sickness. Butch appeared, his little furry face so expressive, so concerned. He whined as if he'd sensed Riley's upset, then crawled up onto his chest and curled up under Riley's chin.

Stupidly enough, it helped.

Emotion clogged Riley's throat, but he hugged Regina with one arm, patted Butch with his other hand, and wished the damn story didn't still hurt so much.

Regina was frozen and silent for a long time before asking, "What ever became of Phil's wife?"

"I stuck around until after the birth, trying to help her out. She had a baby boy she named Phil, after his daddy. Phil had a life insurance policy so she's not too bad off financially. After that, I left. I quit my job and moved here. I heard she got remarried about a year ago. Her kid would be... I dunno, almost five now." He stroked his fingers through Regina's hair, taking comfort in her warmth and softness. "I hope she and the kid are happy."

Suddenly Regina sobbed.

Startled, Riley tried to see her face but she pressed herself so close, it felt like she wanted to crawl inside him. Butch panicked, whining at Riley, poking his nose into Regina's cheek.

"Hey. Honey, what's the matter?"

She hiccuped and in a strangled voice said, "I want to give you something, Riley, okay?"

As she spoke, she turned her face up to his and Riley

grimaced. She didn't cry well. Already her eyes were watery and red, matching her nose. Her cheeks were blotchy. He smiled. "Yeah, sure. But please, don't cry, baby. I can't stand it."

That made her start sobbing again. She crawled out of the bed, still sniffling, and headed out of the room.

"Regina?"

"I'll be right back," she wailed.

Riley watched her go, enjoying the way his shirttails barely covered her tush. He looked at Butch. "Women." Then he added, "But damn, she looks good in my shirt, doesn't she?" And he murmured, "Even better out of it, though."

She came back into the bedroom, the framed photo in her hand. She plopped into bed, burrowed into Riley's side, and dropped the photo on his lap. "Here, you can have it."

Lip curled in distaste, Riley lifted the smug, smiling face of Senator Welling away from his body and dropped it on the nightstand. "Gee, thanks. Just what I always wanted."

Regina gave a choked laugh, lightly punched him, and then hugged him in a strangle hold. "You asked me earlier why I brought the stupid thing along."

Stupid thing? "Uh, yeah."

"I see the photo and I remember his commitment to his family and how he stands for all the things, I value. It gives me hope that someday I'll have those things, too."

Riley rolled his eyes. "Regina..."

"It gave me hope that some day I'd meet a man like him. But I don't need him for inspiration anymore."

She smiled up at Riley and even with the blotchy cheeks, she looked beautiful. "You're the finest man I know, Riley. No one else could ever measure up to you."

Oh hell. It was bad enough when he thought she used Welling as a masculine measuring tape. But if he became the damn tape, she was bound for disappointment. "No, Regina, I'm just a man."

"A good man. A real man. And that's better than a public persona any day."

Riley's heart about stopped. Was it possible she loved him, too? Had he finally gotten through to her? He started to tell her so when his phone rang. Riley reached for the nightstand and snatched up the receiver. "Hello?" And then with foreboding, "Yeah, Dermot. What's up?"

Just as he suspected, Earl had been released. The judge returned not more than a few hours ago, but Earl had made his call and somehow gotten things expedited.

"Thanks for the heads-up. I guess all we can do now is hope he doesn't jump bail." He hung up and rubbed his face. "Looks like we're back to square one unless Senator Welling can remember something vital."

Regina gasped as if someone had pinched her. "Oh no. Senator Welling and the ceremony. We're going to be late."

Riley glanced at the clock and cursed. "We'll make it if we hurry." He threw the covers aside and stood.

Regina remained in bed, her bottom lip caught between her teeth. "Riley? Are you sure we can't just skip it? Somehow, I'm not as excited about seeing him as I had been."

He smiled, caught her under the arms and lifted her from the bed. "No, we can't skip it. I don't want to miss this chance. If we get there early, we can talk to the senator before the ceremony begins and get it out of the way."

"Then come back here and make love some more?"

Riley feigned a scandalized gasp. "Why, Ms. Foxworth, you surprise me."

She grinned. "When we get home, I'll surprise you even more."

Home. He liked the sound of that. "It's a deal."

10

Butch put on an awful, melodramatic fit about being left alone. He was a smart little dog who understood *everything* whenever the mood suited him, and right now he understood that two dressed humans heading for the door meant he'd be alone.

He didn't like it, and he didn't hold back in letting them know his deepest feelings. Not only did he howl pitifully, but he laid flat on his belly and did an army crawl, as if his little legs wouldn't work.

They tried stepping out and waiting to see if he'd calm down. He didn't. He made such a racket that he sounded like a pack of wolves. Riley feared complaints from his neighbors if they left Butch carrying on so enthusiastically.

In the end, since the ceremony would mostly be outdoors, Regina gave in and tucked him away in her satchel. She hooked his leash to his collar as a precaution in case he attempted to escape. She kept the leash wrapped around her hand and the strap of the big bag over her shoulder with Butch close to her side.

He seemed to like that just fine. He curled up and went to sleep like a baby in a knapsack.

"And you said *I'd* spoil him?"

Regina scowled at that accusation. "He's still getting used to us. There's been no stability in his life yet, what with me bringing him home, then bringing him here...."

Riley drew her close without mussing her hair, and pressed a warm kiss to her forehead. "I do understand. Even cantankerous little dogs need reassuring." Then he grinned. "Just remember that us old dogs need it, too."

Regina intended to reassure him in a big way as soon as they returned. She was going to tell him how she felt. Love was love and it should never be denied. To get it, you had to give it. That was the argument she'd used when choosing Butch, and now she'd apply it to Riley. She'd give him her heart and hope he gave his in return.

It had worked with Butch.

Riley drove his truck to the ceremony. Regina felt the difference now in just being with him. There was a new comfort, a new ease that existed between them. She thought of everything he'd told her, everything he'd gone through. No wonder he hadn't wanted to get involved again. He had not only the emotional turmoil of an unfaithful spouse, but he also had a battle with his professional conscience for being untruthful.

Regina considered his thoughtfulness for Phil's wife one of the most commendable things she'd ever heard. Riley had put his own hurt aside to protect someone else—and that, more than anything, defined the type of man he was.

Milling crowds filled the lawn in front of the museum center where the Historical Society had planned the ceremony. Keeping Regina tucked close to his side with a precautionary, proprietary air, Riley repeatedly flashed his badge to dispatch a path to the quiet chambers inside the museum where Senator Welling passed the time until his introduction. In the end though, it was Regina who got them beyond the final barrier of guards.

She gave her name and politely asked them to inform Senator Welling that she would greatly appreciate a moment of his time. One unconvinced guard did as she asked, then returned with a smile, saying Senator Welling would love to see her again.

The guards wouldn't let Riley in, though, and Riley wouldn't let Regina in without him. He was most firm on that issue, so Regina stuck her head in the heavy carved wooden door of the museum's inner sanctum and requested that her escort be given entrance as well.

Senator Welling, smiling and as jovial as the last time she'd seen him, rose from behind a large desk and bid them both inside. "Ms. Foxworth—Regina—how wonderful to see you again."

It was enough of a surprise that he remembered her, but he also sounded sincerely happy to see her. Regina smiled with true pleasure. By rights, the Senator should have looked exhausted from his recent travels. The commendation from the Historical Society came at the tail end of a two-week tour. Instead, he looked vital and energetic. "Senator Welling. I hope we're not imposing."

"Of course not. And please, no formality here. Call me Xavier. After all, we're old friends now."

"Why, thank you. I'd be honored."

Another guard came forward to frisk both her and Riley.

"I'm sorry," Xavier said with a wry, philosophical shrug. "They're quite insistent on doing their jobs."

"Oh, I understand. You're a very important man. Of course they have to protect you." Regina held her arms out to her sides and submitted to being patted down. Butch didn't take it well, snapping at the guard and startling him when he peeked inside the bag. The Senator, a lover of animals, was merely amused when Butch peeked out at him and growled.

Unlike the others who'd called her dog a rat and worse, Xavier said, "Such distinctive coloring. A purebred Chihuahua?"

"Yes, thank you. I think he's beautiful, too." Regina beamed at Xavier for his exquisite taste in animals.

Riley didn't take the invasion of privacy much better than Butch had, but at least he didn't try to bite anyone. He introduced himself, showed his badge, and still got roughly checked for hidden weapons. Regina watched him warily, unsure what he might do.

When the security check had been completed, he merely nodded. "Senator Welling—"

"Xavier, please," he reminded Riley.

Riley conceded with a nod. "Xavier. Thank you for seeing us."

"It's my pleasure." After sharing a hearty handshake with Riley, he took Regina's hand and winked at her. "We have plenty of time to spare before the ceremony and I've only been sitting here hoping I won't trip over my words."

His charming, self-deprecating grin could win over the worst skeptics, Regina decided. "I'm sure you'll keep them all enthralled."

Laughing, still holding her hand, Xavier turned to Riley. "My biggest fan, or so she tells me."

Riley's mouth flattened. "Yeah, she tells me that, too."

Regina frowned at Riley's tone—and noticed he was staring at Xavier's hand clasping hers. Could he be jealous? He'd made that comment about old dogs needing reassurance, too. Trying to be inconspicuous, she pulled away from Xavier. "Senator, how is your intern? That lovely young lady I met at the park with you."

His gray brows rose in confusion. "My intern?"

Regina forged on. "I recall she was very quiet, but you told me she worked hard and was very dedicated to you."

Xavier cleared his throat. "Yes, a hard worker. I'm sorry, but you know, I can't keep up with all the interns. They come and go, and…" Suddenly he stopped. He turned to his guards and said, "Wait outside."

The guards shared a look, hesitant to obey.

Xavier frowned and rounded his desk to shoo them away. "Really, I'm quite safe here with the young lady and her friend. Go. I'd like some privacy."

Regina was stunned at the sudden turn of events. Both men were forced out a door at the back of the office, behind where Xavier had been sitting. In a heartbeat, Riley was there, standing mostly in front of her, blocking her with his body. She tried to nudge him aside, but he wouldn't move.

"Riley, really," she whispered.

Glancing over his shoulder, he gave her one brief, hard look that stopped all other protests in her throat.

When Xavier turned back to them, his expression had become strained. "There. Much better, don't you think?" His smile didn't reach his eyes. "Please, take a seat and tell me what you've been up to." Xavier returned to his chair.

Regina started to take the nearest chair opposite the desk, but Riley stopped her by backing further into her.

"With your permission, Senator, I'd like to ask you a few questions about that day in the park."

Xavier's complexion paled. He looked down at his desk a moment, then faced Riley squarely. "Is there a problem?"

Regina could feel the tension in Riley, but she didn't understand it. He seemed braced for an attack, ready to charge. But why?

"Since that day, Regina has been repeatedly threatened by someone. I believe it started with the car that ran her off the road."

Xavier swallowed, and in a murmur said, "Thank God she wasn't injured that day. Terrible, terrible thing to happen to a young woman. She could have been killed."

Riley's arms hung loose at his sides. It was a negligent pose, but Regina had taken enough lessons from him to know he was readying himself, keeping limber, poised.

"Yes, she could have. And that wasn't the only incident. She's been accosted several times. The worst, however, was the fire."

Xavier's head shot up. "A fire?"

"Yes. A deliberate fire, in my opinion. It burned a

building to the ground and almost took Regina and her friend with it.''

Xavier squeezed his eyes shut and shook his head. "This is dreadful. Just dreadful."

By small degrees, Riley started backing up, forcing Regina toward the door where they'd entered.

The sense of foreboding was so thick in the air, Regina thought she might choke on it. "Senator?"

He shook his head. "I'm only a man, flawed, damn it."

"What the hell does that mean?" Riley demanded.

The senator looked up, then beyond Riley. His face went ashen.

Someone had stepped in the room behind them.

Startled, more than a little frightened, Regina jerked around—and let out a relieved breath. Mrs. Welling stood there, elegantly dressed in a turquoise suit with pearl jewelry.

Riley started to move Regina to his side, but Mrs. Welling reached out and took her hand. ' Hello. I heard Xavier had guests."

Flustered, Regina all but gushed. "Mrs. Welling! It's so wonderful to finally meet you. I didn't know you were here, too, but then you always accompany Xavier, don't you?"

"'Xavier'?" She slanted a sardonic look at her husband. "I see you're a close friend, to call him by his first name."

"Oh." Regina felt the heat pulsing in her face. "No, not at all. He just—"

"It's all right. My husband has mentioned you, Ms. Foxworth." Mrs. Welling was tall, softened with age, but still striking in appearance. Her brown hair was stylishly laced with gray, her eyes a stunning, clear blue. She held Regina's hand overlong.

Regina was aware of Xavier slowly standing behind his desk, of Riley stepping aside so that he stood between husband and wife. Regina prayed Riley wouldn't lose his temper and do something outlandish.

She was trying to send him a warning look to behave when the door behind Xavier opened. Regina's view was blocked by Riley, but she heard him curse. With Mrs. Welling still clasping her hand, she stepped to the side to better see.

A tall man, probably a guard, stood there. He wasn't smiling, and he kept his narrowed, alert gaze on Riley. Slowly he lifted his right arm and pointed a gun.

Regina gasped. Instinctively, she tried to move toward Riley, but Mrs. Welling kept her immobile. "Meet Earl Rochelle, Ms. Foxworth. I believe he's made himself something of a nuisance to you."

Confusion warred with fear. "You...you're the one who broke into my apartment?" Regina had a hard time taking it in. Mrs. Welling seemed so cold, Xavier was rocking back and forth on his heels, muttering to himself and shaking his head. Riley just stood there, as sturdy and unshakable as a stone wall.

Earl nodded at Riley. "Your lover boy roughed me up. But now it's time for payback."

Riley shifted the tiniest bit. "You son of a bitch." His voice was calm, without inflection. "So you're working for the senator?"

Xavier violently shook his head. "No. No, I'd never hurt anyone...."

Mrs. Welling laughed. "Xavier, be truthful. You hurt me all the time." Her lovely face contorted—with pain, with anger. "Every single time you crawl into bed with another woman. But no more, you bloated pompous ass. I've stuck with you this long, and I'll be damned if I let you ruin our family now."

Regina turned to face her, her brain blank with shock, with disbelief. "Mrs. Welling... I'm sorry. I didn't know."

"Of course you didn't. Along with a good portion of the constituents, you think Xavier is an honorable man, a *family* man. In truth, my dear, he's a lying cheating pig."

Xavier shook his head, his face now bright pink, his eyes pleading. "No, dear. It was only those few times...."

"I'm not a fool, Xavier. I've known of every single affair. Your intern—who by the way, Ms. Foxworth, is no more than a well-paid prostitute—was only one in a long line of young women. You preach family values, all the while you're paying for sex with a common whore."

Her voice had risen with her ire, and Earl moved closer. "Mrs. Welling, please. Discretion is necessary."

She released Regina to wave away his concerns. "I dismissed the guards for now. I told them to return when it's time for Xavier's introduction. We've at least fifteen more minutes."

Regina suddenly understood. "The photograph." She stared at Mrs. Welling. "It has the intern... I mean, the prostitute, in the picture with the senator. They were..." Aghast, she turned to stare at Xavier. "They were having an affair *in the park?*"

"You begin to understand. The stupid park wasn't due to be open. Xavier knew I was watching him, and he thought he could lose my spies in the woods. But Earl kept a tail on him." She glanced at her husband with loathing. "Earl saw everything, including the damn picture you took. Xavier, the idiot, didn't think it was anything to worry about. He didn't think anyone would put two and two together. I know better. If that picture got out, the whole family would be ruined. I had Earl run you off the road, but you kept the camera around your neck and Xavier came to your aid."

Sadly, his shoulders slumped, Xavier said, "I couldn't let you hurt her."

"The way you hurt me?" Mrs. Welling turned away from him. "At the fire we finally got the camera, but it was filled with new film. Since then, we've been unable to find either the undeveloped film or the photograph."

Riley laughed. "She has it framed and keeps it in her bedside drawer."

Regina gaped at him even as she felt herself enveloped in mortified heat. *"Riley."*

Riley ignored her, moving closer to the desk, casually leaning a hip on the edge. Earl stiffened, but kept quiet.

The senator stared at her in astonishment.

Mrs. Welling's face contorted. "So you've slept with him, too?" she wrongly concluded. Outraged, she shook her head and addressed Riley. "Thank you for letting us know." Her lip curled, destroying her image of a respected and elegant politician's wife. "Retrieving the vile thing will be so much easier now, especially with you two out of the picture."

"And how exactly do you plan to accomplish that?"

At Riley's question, she pulled another gun out of her purse, but this one was odd-shaped, unlike any gun Regina had ever seen. "Why don't you let me worry about that, Mr. Moore?"

Riley shifted again. Regina felt sure he planned to do something, but what, she couldn't guess. She only wished he'd hurry up. She was starting to sweat nervously. Things did not look good. She realized that she should have been worried about him, but she somehow knew he'd handle things.

Then Mrs. Welling made the bad decision to grab Regina by the hair. She had the odd gun raised when suddenly Butch exploded from the bag with such a feral, wild snarl it sounded like a pack of demon dogs had been unleashed.

He bit Mrs. Welling's hand, her arm, and ran right up to her face where he sank his small sharp teeth into her nose. The woman screamed in reaction and swatted at the dog.

Regina saw red. She hadn't realized she'd learned anything substantial from Riley, but without any real thought she caught her small dog in one arm, grabbed the arm holding the gun in the other and deftly tripped Mrs. Welling to her back. The woman hit her head on the hardwood floor and stayed there, dazed.

Regina jerked the gun from her hand.

Almost at the same time, Riley moved with blinding

speed. His leg came up and over the desk, landing his foot squarely in the senator's face. He went down with a grunt. Earl moved, but Riley already had the advantage. He grabbed Earl's gun arm, pulled him forward and delivered his elbow into his throat.

Gagging and gasping, Earl collapsed to his knees. The gun fell from his hand and Riley kicked it aside. Hesitating only a moment to make certain Earl was sufficiently incapacitated, Riley turned and reached for the fallen gun. Both doors exploded open as guards filed in. Riley groaned, his hands lifted in a nonthreatening pose. He started to explain, and finally saw that Dermot and Lanny headed up the cavalry. He actually laughed.

Dermot grinned. "We followed him. You seemed so sure he was up to something more than a break-in."

Lanny nodded. "And you being sure made us sure, so when the judge returned and we had to release him, we decided it might be smart to keep a close watch."

"Good job," Riley told them and they both puffed up like proud peacocks.

"Explaining to these guys wasn't easy though." Dermot nodded to the hired guards with a scowl.

They ignored him.

One stepped forward and picked up the strange gun by Mrs. Welling. "A tranquilizer gun?"

Regina's knees felt suddenly weak. She trembled from her head to her toes. "She was going to use it on us." Her voice was little more than a breathy squeak. "Then he—" she pointed to Earl "—was going to kill us."

The guards looked at her like she was nuts. Earl

shouted denials. Senator Welling stirred just in time for a small bespectacled woman in a black suit to duck her head into the room and say, "Senator, it's time for...your...introduction." Her eyes rounded, looking huge behind her glasses.

One of the guards caught her arm and pulled her completely into the room, then shut and locked the door.

The senator moaned. Mrs. Welling, now sitting on the floor holding her head, said, "Forget it. There'll be no more honors for him."

Regina looked around at the chaos and wanted to cry. It was more than just the scandal that was sure to ensue, the political ramifications, the threat to her and Riley. Something she'd cherished, something she'd believed was real, had just been defiled in the worst possible way.

Her stomach actually cramped. She'd been such an utter fool.

Then Riley was there, his hand closing gently on her upper arm. "Babe, you're crushing Butch. Loosen up."

Regina glanced at Butch, at his bulgy little eyes, and saw it was true. She relinquished her hold on him.

"That's it. Here, let me hold him." Riley balanced the dog in one arm, up close to his chest because Butch seemed more than a little rattled by all that had happened. He was curled in on himself, his eyes still wild, and low growls continually emitted from deep in his throat as he watched everyone and everything. Once Riley held him, he looked less threatened.

With his other arm, Riley gathered Regina protectively into his side. Regina knew everyone was looking at her with varying degrees of expression—virulence from Mrs. Welling, disgrace from Xavier, concern from Lanny and Dermot.

She felt like a spectacle, something she detested, a feeling left over from her childhood. Ashamed, she turned into Riley to hide. "You told them where I kept the picture."

At her agonized whisper, he tightened his hold and his voice became hard. "Only to distract them, to keep them talking until I could best situate myself to react."

"Oh." She supposed that made sense. She'd put them into a situation and he'd had to rescue them because of it.

"Damn it, Red, I would never deliberately do anything to hurt you."

He sounded so outraged, Regina tried to soothe him. "Okay, Riley." The last thing she wanted was another spectacle.

To her surprise, Riley murmured near her ear, "Red, you've made me so proud."

"Proud?" She wasn't expecting that and her laugh was bitter and hurt. "I was a gullible idiot."

"No. You handled yourself well, disarming Mrs. Welling, protecting Butch, helping me."

Had she done all that? She had struck out at the crazy woman, but... "I got us in this situation in the first place by being an idiot."

"No." He turned her to face him, his expression volatile. "You're you, sweet and trusting and sincere, and I happen to love you an awful lot."

She jerked back. The suffocating crowd and her own embarrassment seemed to fade away. Her entire focus was on Riley and those awesome words he'd just uttered. "You what?"

With exasperation, he took her arm and towed her into the farthest corner of the room. It wasn't really far enough, merely a few feet away. The guards were watching them while another phoned a supervisor on his cell phone. The situation was sticky and could explode into an ugly scandal if it wasn't handled quickly and efficiently.

Riley cupped the back of her neck and put his forehead to hers. "Listen to me, Regina. I know the human garbage that exists in our world. Hell, I've dealt with them more times than I care to remember. Rapists, murderers, sadists... They're out there and we all have to be careful. But there are a lot of good people in the world, too, the kind of people you believe in."

"Like you."

"Like *you*." He looked pained. "I'm not perfect, Red. I'm as flawed as your senator. But I would never cheat on you or deliberately hurt you and I'll always try to make you happy. You have my word on that."

She stared at him.

"I love you for who you are. I don't want you to change, to be jaded by this. I *like* the things you believe in. Hell, I believe in them, too." He bent to see her face. "You still do, don't you? You won't let one creep distort things for you?"

Her smile came slowly, along with sudden insight. The senator wasn't the man she'd believed him to be— but Riley was. True, he wasn't perfect, so he'd likely make mistakes in his life, just as she would. But he was steadfast, solid, a man you could rely on

A man she could trust with her love.

"No, I won't let him disillusion me." She touched Riley's chest. She knew Riley, so she knew how incredible a person could be. No one could ever change that. "I love you, too, Riley. I fought it, but I knew last night that I'd lost the battle."

He didn't smile, but new warmth darkened his blue eyes. "I've known how I feel for a long while now."

"Buck and Harris and Ethan knew how you felt, too."

"They *what?*"

Nodding, Regina said, "They told me, but I didn't really believe them." Then in a barely there whisper, she confessed, "I thought you only wanted sex."

He rolled his eyes. "Of course I want sex," he answered in the same low whisper, and then added with gentle awe, "Look at you."

At his very private words, she glanced around the room. She knew no one could hear him, but when Lanny winked at her, she blushed. They really should have found some privacy for this chat.

"I was giving you time, Red, and trying to get this mess sorted out so we wouldn't be distracted." He looked up at the sound of the door opening and two more men—very official in appearance—stepped in. "I think the mess just got messier, but at least you're out of it now. I can concentrate on you."

"On us?" she specified.

He pressed a firm kiss to her mouth. "Yes."

"I do love you, Riley, but now that this is over, I have no reason to stay with you. I'm not the type of woman who shacks up."

He went stiff as a board, and Regina said, "Will you marry me?"

He slumped against her, half in relief, half in amusement. Butch complained until he could squirrel up between their bodies and poke his face out.

"Riley?" Regina prayed he'd said yes.

"Yeah, I'll marry you." He grinned. "It's nice having a very proper woman around. Takes the guesswork out of things."

With that settled, Regina turned back to face the room. "What do you think will happen now?"

"I dunno. I don't really care as long as none of them can ever again threaten you."

A sort of wistful melancholy crept up on her. "It's strange, but I still think he's a good senator—he's just not a good husband."

"Maybe. I promise I'll be a good husband." When she smiled in agreement, Riley hugged her tight. "One thing, Red."

"What?"

"You remember what I said about babies?"

Regina softened all the way to her toes. Her knees felt like butter, her heart full and ripe. "Yes."

"I'm a homebody at heart. I want a house—"

"I have the house," she rushed to remind him, just in case he was getting cold feet.

"—and a dog."

"Got the dog, too. A perfect dog. A dog others will envy." She rubbed Butch's oversized ears.

Laughing, Riley hefted Butch up closer to his face and the dog playfully nipped his chin, appearing very pleased with the situation. "I'd really like a few kids *without* tails if you think we can manage that sometime in the misty future."

Tears filled her eyes. All around them was chaos, but the government could work itself out. This was important. "Since we love each other and we're getting married, and we intend to stay married forever, I'd say it would only be right and proper."

RILEY STEPPED through the door, took one look at Regina, and backed out. With the music she had playing on the stereo, she hadn't heard him. He turned to his friends and said, "Wait out here a second."

Buck crossed his arms over his massive chest. "If you're going to leave me hanging in the street just so you can grab a nooner, forget it."

Harris laughed. "Men in love are so predictable."

Rosie shoved him for that inelegant remark. "You'll get yours someday, Harris. Just wait and see."

His horrified expression had both Riley and Ethan chuckling.

Shaking his head, Riley said, "No, it's not that. She's just not ready for you. Two minutes, I swear. That's all I need."

"Two minutes? Talk about a quickie," Harris muttered, then ducked behind Buck before Rosie could reach him.

Riley slipped through the door and locked it behind him. He loved the house that Regina had chosen. It wasn't all that large but it had a real family feel to it, a coziness that she enhanced by her mere presence.

Since she'd already taken care of a sizeable down payment, he'd splurged on most of the furnishings. Between their combined efforts, things were really coming together.

The music continued to play, and Regina still had her delectable rump in the air as she rummaged beneath the couch for Butch's bone. The dog sat beside her, his expression anxious and watchful.

"Can I help?"

She screeched, whipped around to sit on her butt, and stared at him. "You're home early!"

"It ended quicker than I thought." He'd had to testify in court on a burglary, then had stopped by to see his friends. They'd invited themselves over, but obviously Regina wasn't ready for company.

Before he could explain that he had them all with him, she was on her feet and racing Butch to the door to greet him. Both woman and dog appeared thrilled with his arrival.

Dressed in one of his shirts—something she knew he loved seeing—and with her rich hair wound into enormous curlers around her head, Regina launched herself into his arms. Since that day at the Historical Society, she'd grown completely at ease with him. Around others, she remained immeasurably polite and proper, but with Riley she shared every facet of herself, including her less polished moments. Like now.

When the delicious kiss ended, Butch demanded his attention with a yodeling bark. He stretched up to stand on his hind legs, dancing around in what Riley called his circus dog impersonation.

Riley picked him up and treated him to a full body rub before saying to Regina, "Sorry to break it to you, but everyone is with me."

Her hands went to her cheeks and her green eyes widened. "Everyone?"

He nodded toward the door. "Harris and Buck, Rosie and Ethan. They invited themselves over. They're waiting on the porch."

The words no sooner left his mouth than she whipped around and dashed down the hallway to their bedroom. Riley enjoyed the back view of her, watching her long legs and the way his shirttails bounced over her bottom. "I'll keep them entertained while you finish getting ready."

The slamming of the door was her only reply.

Fifteen minutes later Regina emerged dressed in pressed slacks, a beige cotton sweater and a huge smile. "Sorry I kept you all waiting. Usually I'm dressed and ready by this time of the day, but I got behind this morning after Barbara Walter's people called."

Rosie's mouth fell open. Ethan jerked around to face her. Buck, who'd been on the floor playing with Butch, froze. Harris snorted in disbelief.

Riley, the only one with his wits still about him, raised a brow. "Barbara Walters?" He wasn't all that surprised. It seemed everyone in the media wanted the scoop on Senator Welling's sudden withdrawal. With his influence, the senator had put a gag order on the entire event. The guards present that day would never speak a word. Lanny and Dermot had been warned that they could lose their jobs if they released any information to the press.

Riley had assured the senator's people up front that they couldn't use his job to threaten him. All he cared about was that Regina be kept safe. Beyond that stipulation, they could handle the situation as quietly and secretively as they wished. But they *would* have to handle it because he wouldn't tolerate any more threats to Regina. So far, they had things in hand.

Regina was the only one left that could talk—and she wasn't about to.

"What did she want?" Buck asked.

"The same thing the others wanted."

Agog with fascination, Rosie asked, "To hear firsthand what happened with the senator?"

"Right." Regina sat down on Riley's lap, which was the only seat available in the small living room. She leaned back against his chest and smiled. "I told them that they'd just have to find out the nitty-gritty details like everyone else, after the federal investigation ended."

Rosie flopped back against her husband's arm. "Wow. Barbara Walters and you turned her down."

Buck rolled to his back and propped up on his elbows. "I can't believe you don't want revenge after the hell Welling's wife put you through."

Regina shrugged. "What good would revenge do? The senator has lost a lot of credibility with his constituents. They apparently don't like secrets, but with his wife under indictment and his own blame in the whole thing, what else can he do but keep quiet?"

"He could have not cheated in the first place," Harris grouched with feeling, then looked blank when everyone stared at him. "What? I have morals, too, ya know."

Regina sighed. "They have two children, and I think

the kids have been through enough. Even with his wife blaming everything on Earl, her involvement is bound to make headlines eventually. The whole family is going to suffer. I won't take part in that."

Harris nodded, giving her a look full of admiration. "You're something else, Regina, you know that?"

Riley scowled at his tender tone, but Harris blew it by saying, "And here I thought you were a nosy reporter."

"I am." Regina gave them all an evil grin. "But I still like the more personal and upbeat human-interest stories." She hesitated just long enough to add impact, then announced, "That's why I told Walter's retinue that if they wanted a real scoop they should bring their TV crew to Chester and check out the local heroes."

Riley choked on his own breath.

Ethan groaned as if in mortal pain.

"You'd never get them here for something like that," Rosie said. "They like stories of worldwide appeal."

"Oh, I dunno. What could be more appealing to the world than the local heroes who keep us safe?" She slanted Rosie a look. "I specifically mentioned Harris and Buck."

Buck bolted upright. "I'm no hero! Hell, I just own a lumberyard."

"You were right there by Riley the day he caught Earl. You may not have a hero's occupation, but you have the soul of a hero."

"I don't!"

"Yes, you do," she insisted. "Think of the interview as free advertising for your business."

Harris said, *"Oh gawd,"* with great disgust. "That's weak, Regina. Very weak."

She didn't seem the least upset by the criticism. "When I told them two of the men were still single, they sounded pretty interested. They told me they're doing this whole segment on singles in America, and heroes would naturally be prime fodder for the piece. They want me to call them back with more information."

Buck and Harris stared at each other, their Adam's apples bopping in panic.

"You wouldn't."

"You didn't."

Riley started to laugh. "I can tell you unequivocally that she would. For some insane reason she thinks the two of you epitomize all that is good in mankind."

"They're your and Ethan's friends," Regina said with prim regard. "And you two are definitely heroic."

"Hear, hear," Rosie agreed.

"So of course they're good men. And since they won't let me interview them..." She left the sentence dangling with loaded suggestion.

"Hey, I put up with it," Ethan pointed out.

"Me, too," Riley added. His own interview had been carefully edited by Regina. Anything that might have been too personal or hurtful had been omitted.

It was still embarrassing, especially because the love she felt for him had shone through and Harris and Buck had harassed him for days afterward, pretending to swoon, blowing him kisses and asking for his autograph. But the public had gobbled it up, his chief was thrilled with the positive P.R. for the department and

Regina had thanked him oh so sweetly, so he was glad he'd given in.

Buck finally said, "Regina, be reasonable. You have to call off Walters."

Her nose lifted. "I could do that—*if* you agree to give me a story." Her gaze slanted to Harris. "Both of you."

With hardy groans and a lot of grumbling, they surrendered to the inevitable. "Deal."

Regina relaxed. "I'll return their call after dinner. But I need the interviews before our wedding next week."

"Why the rush?" Harris asked, looking somewhat stricken by the whole idea of being in the limelight.

"After the wedding, I plan to be busy for a while— with my own personal hero."

Riley hugged her close. He knew the truth: Regina was the heroic one. With her big heart and unwavering faith in human nature, she had filled his soul. He intended to keep her safe for the rest of their lives. If that made him a hero, too, at least in her eyes, then he'd gladly live with the label.

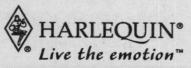

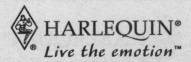